Buckley: Encouraged to Pray

The Barnabas Chronicles
Book 11

By

Ronna M. Bacon

Jeremiah 29:12
Then you will call on me and come and pray to me,
and I will listen to you.

Hebrews 4:16
Let us then approach God's throne of grace with
confidence, so that we may receive mercy and find
grace to help us in our time of need.
NKJV

Table of Contents

Feeling as if he was standing at the crossroads of his life, Buckley Cullen stared through the windshield of his car, not seeing the scenery in front of him. He had drawn to the side of the road and into a little store parking lot, not really wanting anything, but feeling he was lost and needing some help. Just what kind of help that was, he wasn't sure. He was worn out, he thought. He had needed a break and the church board had agreed. The pastor was important to them, they told him. The two weeks that he had asked for had been freely granted.

Buckley shoved open the door of his car and then stood beside it, looking around. He had not gone too far from home, taking trips by the day, or just staying home. Today, a Sunday, he had driven away early in the morning, not wanting to see the sympathy on his friends' faces. They were a tight-knit group, the fourteen men of the Barnabas Foundation. Even with ten of them now married, they still stood with one another in difficulties. And there had been great difficulties, Buckley thought, some almost losing their lives.

Hearing a commotion from behind him, Buckley spun around and then moved to the other side of his car, watching closely as the young lady, around his age he thought, ran around the corner of the building. He frowned as he saw the fear on her face and then raised his eyes to watch the man chasing her. Buckley moved quickly forward, reaching for her arm and tucking her behind him, standing with his feet spread apart in a protective manner, his fists curled at his sides.

"Hey! What's the problem here?" Buckley's question and his sudden appearance stopped the man in his tracks.

"Get out of my way! That's my woman!" The man glared at Buckley, who simply stood, not moving, not speaking.

Buckley could feel the lady's head moving against his back in a negative manner. He spoke quietly to her.

"Is that the truth?"

"No." Her voice was low. "It's not. It never has been. Can you help me?"

"Certainly. My car's unlocked. Head for it and lock yourself in. I'll stall him somehow."

"Good luck with that!"

He heard her mutter even as he felt her moving away from him and then the click of the car door. His eyes never moved from the man in front of him, so he saw the instant that the man's fist came his way. He ducked, his foot going out to trip the man, who tumbled to the ground and lay still. Buckley was on the move, into his car and backing it out on the road and disappearing with a trail of dust. He caught a glimpse of the man in his rearview mirror through the dust, a fist raised in anger at him.

Driving away rapidly, Buckley chose roads that he knew would lead him home before he pulled over into a picnic area at the side of the road. He turned to the young woman and stopped, mesmerized by her beauty. Her hair, he thought, is the red-gold of a fiery sunset. Her eyes when she looked up at him were the curiously-coloured jade of a canal near his home. He could see the fear in her eyes and the uncertainty that flickered there as well.

Buckley pulled out his wallet and found one of his cards, handing it to her.

"You're safe with me. I'm a pastor in a nearby town." He looked back towards the road. "What was that all about?"

The lady took the card, her finger gently tracing his name. "Buckley Cullen. A strange name for a minister."

Buckley grinned, his teeth showing white against the redness of his neatly trimmed beard and moustache before he ran a hand through his reddish-blond hair. His dark brown eyes studied her more closely.

"You're scared."

"Well, yeah! He's not going to ever give up." She slumped back against the door. "I'm Locklin Dinneen. Thank you for rescuing me, but I have to go back. At least, I think that I do."

"And why would that be?"

"Because it's my home. I have nowhere else to go. And so far, no one has lifted a hand to help me."

—

"Explain, please?" Buckley was concerned, knowing that if he returned the lady, she would face difficulties that he suddenly wanted to spare her from.

"That monster? He's Len Forester. He's been trying to make me his girl or whatever he wants to call it since I was a teenager. I avoid him, stay in crowds, lock myself in my home. It has not stopped him."

"And the police? What have they said?"

"I haven't been able to go to them. It would be my word against his. In this area? His family is the one who counts. Mine didn't." Her voice was barely audible as she finished.

"That's not right. I can help you. I have a number of friends who will as well." Buckley started the car again and moved back to the road, heading for home. "I work for the Barnabas Foundation, even though I have a church near there. They will take you in and protect you."

"No one can, Mr. Cullen. I'll sorry, but no one has ever been able to." Locklin blinked rapidly before she screamed.

Buckley shot a look towards her, seeing the truck heading his way. He spun the wheel, heading for the other side of the road, hitting the gravel and losing control. His car hit the ditch and rolled, ending up against a tree, dust, and debris flying through the air before it became to float gently to the ground.

The man paused his truck's forward advance and then drove rapidly away. He would return, pretending to be a Good Samaritan, he thought. Give them about thirty minutes and he would be back. This was a little travelled road, that he knew. It had been perfect for what he had done.

Buckley roused from where he had slumped against the wheel, batting at the deflated airbag to clear his way. He groaned, a hand to his shoulder before he squinted. This is not good, he thought. What did I go and do, that I don't remember going and doing? Hearing a soft moan, he spun, his seatbelt releasing under his fingers. He stared at the young woman, finally remembering their conversation.

"Locklin? Can you hear me? Locklin?" He reached for her, releasing her from her seatbelt. His fingers touched the large lump on the side of her head, blood oozing from it. When she didn't respond, he shifted once more, shoving at his door until he could finally open it. He reached to gently pull her from the vehicle, cradling her against him as he stood. He was scared, Buckley admitted to himself. He was out in the wilds, or so it seemed, his car was wrecked, and he had an injured lady in his arms.

Buckley stared up at the road and then around him, before moving towards a more sheltered area. Scanning the sky, he shook his head. It was spring, granted, but the clouds were moving in. Laying Locklin down, he staggered back to his car, working to open the trunk and find the blanket he kept there. He would need it. He returned to wrap her in it, sitting and cradling her to him, her head on his shoulder. Finding his phone in his pocket, Buckley stared at it, praying that he would have service before he dialled a friend's number.

—

Buckley began to pray, an ingrained habit of his. He begged God to protect the lady that he held, his interest already piqued. He prayed for their safety, that the man would be kept away. He begged God that Burnie would arrive quickly. His eyes studied Locklin's white face, and he was afraid, afraid that he had hurt her when he moved her. Please, God? Heal this lady. Don't let me have hurt her.

Chapter 2

Buckley tucked his phone away once more, his arms tightening around Locklin. She had not stirred, the dark lashes laying on her ivory cheeks. His head down on hers, he thought through the conversation that he had just had with his friend, Burnie.

Burnie had been shocked, to say the least, at the call from Buckley but had readily agreed to come and find him. He would also arrange for a tow truck, he said. Just where was he anyway?

Buckley had given a short bark of laughter. "I was on my way home and someone ran me off the road. I need transportation, Burnie. Can you help? Right at the moment, my own car is up against a tree and isn't about to be driven."

Burnie had been silent for a moment before his cautious voice sounded through the phone. "Buckley, are you having one of those adventures?"

"What do you mean?" Buckley had a good idea what Burnie was asking.

"You know. Those adventures. The ones that our friends have had. The ones we told Brody ended with him? Are you? Because if you are, I'm telling the others. I don't care if it's Sunday or not, and you're not behind the pulpit. I'm telling."

Buckley gave a brief bark of laughter. "Go ahead and tell. It appears that I am. I rescued a lady in distress and got run off the road for my troubles."

"Are you okay? What about your car? Obviously, it's not working if you're calling me for help." Buckley could hear the door slam as Burnie ran out of his apartment.

"The car is likely totalled. I'll need a tow. Dan would come. This is about where I was. As to the lady?" Buckley stared down at her. "Right now, she's unconscious. I just pray that I didn't hurt her when I pulled her out of the car."

"Whose side?"

"What do you mean? Whose side?"

"Whose side got the brunt of it?"

"Hers. The car rolled when I hit gravel. I ended up against a tree. Is Brady around?"

"He is. He's with me as is Bradon. We're on our way. Stay safe, Buckley." Burnie dropped his phone, staring at his friends even as he drove away from the building that they all called home, each with their own apartments.

"What was that all about? You dragged us with you, Burnie. I know that you don't do that without cause." Brady shared a look with Bradon.

"Buckley's been in an accident. He has a lady with him who he says is unconscious. He asked for you, Brady."

"Buckley? And a lady? He's having an adventure?" Bradon shook his head. "I didn't expect him to be the next one."

"Who did you expect then?" Burnie turned towards the road that Buckley had indicated. He knew that had a ways to go, but he was proceeding just as quickly as he could. He could see a tow truck behind him. "Is that Dan?"

"It is. And we expected it to be you." Brady grinned at the look of horror that Burnie pretended. "Your lady is out there, Burnie. Not in one of those books you write."

"Yeah, those books. No readers would ever believe your stories if I ever wrote them."

"Maybe someday, you should. God protected us, led us, brought our ladies and us together, and through it all, showed just what a great God we have." Bradon paused, his thoughts on his own bride. Ennis was truly a blessing sent by God, he thought, the perfect one for him.

"Yeah. Maybe." Burnie finally slowed. "This looks as if there's been some trouble." He pulled to a stop on the shoulder of the road.

"There." Brady was out of the car, running towards Buckley's vehicle. "Not here. Where are they?"

The three men stared around before Bradon pointed. "There. Under those trees. He's hidden them."

Brady dropped to his knees beside Buckley, a hand on his friend's shoulder, even as they heard Dan beginning to work around Buckley's car.

"We'll have to report this." Bradon walked back towards Dan, who nodded at his shouted request. He turned back. "Dan's already done it. Wherever Buckley was, he's in provincial territory."

"Buckley?" Burnie had dropped down by his friend. "Can you hear us?"

"I can. You can stop shouting." Buckley squinted up at them, his headache raging. "You're here. Good. Locklin needs help."

Locklin had roused not long before his friends had arrived. Buckley had questioned her, searched her eyes, but had little response from her other than her statement that her head hurt. And just who was he? He shouldn't be holding her, she stated.

He had simply held her tighter, worry on his face. His prayers were raising but for once, he wasn't sure that they were being heard. He was scared for the lady in his arms. Buckley had kept constant vigil, worried that the man after her would find them and take her, with him not able to protect or shield her.

"We need to call an ambulance, Buckley. She needs to be in a hospital." Brady was busy examining her. "She'll need X-Rays of that lump at the very least." Brady was a paramedic, and very concerned.

"No. No hospital. Not here." Locklin struggled to stand, subsiding back down at Buckley's arms tightened on her.

"No, not here. We'll take you to my town. Doc, a friend, is working today. He'll look after you." Buckley looked past the three men to watch the red and blue lights of the patrol vehicle that had stopped. "Fellows, can we get to your car? I don't want her out in the open any more than we have to."

"She's in danger." Bradon reached to help Buckley stand, not questioning his statement. "Let's get you situated in Burnie's car. You'll need to talk to the police."

"I know." Buckley gently set Locklin down, shifting her to the middle of the seat, and fastening her seatbelt. "I'll be right back, Locklin. I'm just going to talk with the officer." He watched as fear whitened her face. "My friends will be here. No one will get to you. I promise you that. God is watching out for you."

Locklin closed her eyes against the pain even as she gave a brief nod. "Please, Buckley. Be careful."

Buckley finally walked back towards his friends, his body hurting in so many places. He could barely keep himself upright. Brady's hand was there to steady him as he approached them.

"All set?"

Buckley nodded, even as he slipped to the seat beside Locklin. "We are. He'll track us down, he said, just to finalize our statements. Locklin?" Buckley bent his head to study her and then wrapped an arm around her. "Let's move, fellows. I feel someone watching us."

Chapter 3

Doc peered over his reading glasses as he heard the footsteps approaching him in the Emergency Department of the local hospital and then was on his feet, moving towards his young friends.

"Brady? You're not working today."

"No, I'm not. Buckley has had an accident. He needs to be assessed. He has a young lady with him as well. She's taken a hard blow to the head. She's somewhat disoriented." Brady pointed to Locklin.

"In here, Buckley. Set your lady on the bed." Doc pointed to the door. "And you head for the next room."

"Sorry, Doc. I can't leave her. Someone threatened her and I can't let her be by herself." Buckley planted his feet near the stretcher, finding Locklin's hand reaching for his. "This is Locklin Dinneen, Doc. We were in an accident, rolling my car, and her side ended up against the tree. She was unconscious for a while."

His three friends headed for the waiting room, Brady's phone out to call their employer, Barnabas Carey, of the Barnabas Foundation. He squinted at the clock and groaned. He would be in church.

"Brady? What's wrong? You never call me during church." Barnabas had stepped from the sanctuary, to pace outside.

"It's Buckley. He's here in the hospital, after an accident. And he has a young lady with him, a Locklin Dinneen."

"He was? He does? How is he?" Barnabas headed for his truck, knowing that he might well be needed.

"He says that he hurts. Likely bumps and bruises." Brady shared a look with Bradon. "It's the lady, Barnabas. Apparently, he rescued her and they were run off the road. I don't have many details."

"Okay. On my way. Doc's there?"

"He is. He tried to make Buckley leave but he's refusing to leave her side." Brady suppressed a grin. "He sounds the rest of us."

"Like that?" Barnabas shook his head. "He's fallen already, just like all of you. Love at first sight and all. Okay. See you in ten."

Doc turned to Buckley, making him sit, pulling the curtain around the stretcher where Locklin lay.

"Buckley, I need to assess you. Locklin will need some X-Rays at the very minimum. Do you know who her next of kin is?"

Buckley sighed. "No. We just met. I saved her from a brute. He ran us off the road, is my guess. He was determined that she not escape from him. I couldn't let him have her. Not if I could prevent it, Doc." Buckley kept his eyes on the curtain, not seeing the compassion and concern in his friend's eyes.

"That is all well and good, Buckley, but let me look you over. Were you unconscious?"

"Briefly. I have a headache."

"I'm sure you do." Doc finally moved away, watching as the stretcher bearing Locklin returned. "Stay put, young man. I'll let you know when you can see your lady again."

Buckley nodded, not catching Doc's words, looking up as Barnabas appeared at his side.

"Buckley? You okay?"

"I am. It's Locklin. I'm not sure if she is." Buckley resisted for a moment as Barnabas reached to draw him to his feet. "I need to stay, Barnabas."

"No, you want to stay. Come with me. We need to talk." Barnabas kept his hand on Buckley's shoulder, directing him to the waiting room. "The fellows have left. So, it's you and me and Breck. Talk to us."

Buckley explained just what had transpired, his eyes not leaving the doors to the exam rooms. He didn't see the looks of concern shared between the two men with him.

"Buckley?" Breck waited until Buckley looked at him. "Just what were your plans?"

Buckley shrugged, his finger rubbing at his forehead. "I wasn't thinking, I guess. I just wanted to help her, get her away from him. She said he's been after her since she was a teenager. He called her "his woman". No one addresses a lady like that."

"No, they don't. Not gentleman. Does she have any family?"

"From how she spoke, I would say no. And she did tell me that she couldn't go to the police. That his family were prominent in the area and would be believed over her."

Breck nodded. "Then, we set her up in the apartment near you for now. Just until we can sort through all this." He looked up as an officer approached. "Bill? You're here?"

"I am. I just need to talk to Buckley. Buckley? What happened today?" Bill sat near him, taking notes. "Do you know that you were accused of interfering in a domestic situation?"

"There was no domestic situation. She was terrified, Bill. She was running from him. Locklin told me that she wanted nothing to do with him, and he wouldn't leave her alone." Buckley looked at him. "You believe me, don't you?"

"I do. We know of that family and in particular that man. This is not the first accusation of that sort against him. We just haven't been able to prove anything. The ladies retract their statements or disappear." He looked towards the exam rooms. "I need to talk to her. Buckley, just where are you going?"

"With you. She needs me." Buckley walked away from him, looking for Locklin.

"This is Buckley?" Bill shook his head. "Don't tell me. Adventure number eleven."

Breck and Barnabas shared a look. "It would appear so. He's very protective of her. More so than any of the others, and they have been protective of their ladies."

"I know. Let me go see what I can find out. I take it she'll be at the Foundation building?"

"That's correct. Until we can sort out what's happened and where she wants to be." Breck turned away, heading for the door, intent of talking to Anna, Doc's wife, and setting up the apartment for Locklin. "Barnabas, I'll have some of the ladies find some clothes for her. I doubt that she had time to pack."

"Not likely." Barnabas pulled out his phone. "Breck, wait. I just got a message from the police. It appears that the apartment that she had? The building just exploded. There's nothing left."

Breck spun, shock on his face. "What? Just how close was Buckley to not surviving?"

"That's what we need to find out. The authorities will want to talk with her." Barnabas began to pace. "What was Buckley doing there?"

"I have no idea. He's just been lost the last week or so, staying home or going out on his own for the day." Breck sighed. "He'll need to prove that he wasn't involved."

"That is true. And his heart is already involved." Barnabas nodded to the door. "Head off. Do what you need to. I'll touch base with Will Peters, the chief, and see what we need to do. He'll need legal representation."

Chapter 4

Locklin stared at Buckley, a frown on her face before her eyes slid closed. He waited for her to rouse, finally reaching for the chair near him to sit. She hadn't reacted when the officer had asked her what had happened that day, simply shaking her head. That had concerned Buckley. It had concerned him, even more, when Barnabas had appeared, to let him know that her apartment had been destroyed in an explosion, and just what was he doing in that village, anyway?

Locklin finally roused, reaching to raise the head of her bed, waiting for her eyes to clear from the vertigo that attacked her. Her hand rested on her abdomen, willing the nausea to stop. Her eyes found Buckley, and wonder grew within her. Just who is he, she wondered? Do I know him?

Buckley looked up, a smile lighting his face. "You're awake. How are you feeling?"

"I really don't know. My head hurts and I don't know why. And just who are you?"

"You were in an accident. I stepped in to stop a man from taking you away and he ran us off the road. I'm Buckley Cullen, a minister. You don't remember?"

"No, I'm sorry." Her voice was low, melodious, sounding like a song to his ears. "I'm... I'm.... I can't remember my name. Just who am I?" Panic began to run through her until Buckley's hand found hers.

"You're Locklin Dinneen. We met earlier today." He looked around. "You don't remember what happened?"

"No, I'm sorry. I should leave, though." She sat up, her legs swinging to the side of the bed. She stared at the blood on her T-shirt. "I need to change."

"We can manage that. I have transportation waiting for us. We'll take you to the Foundation building and get you set up there." Buckley helped her to stand, an arm tight around her as he walked them to the back entrance of the department, knowing his friends would be waiting there.

Barnabas watched the couple approach him, exchanging a look with Brady, who had returned, Ennis waiting with them.

"She's not in good shape. She shouldn't be leaving here." Ennis was concerned, to say the least.

"No, but Doc can watch her. He wants her with them. Anna's preparing a room for them." Barnabas walked towards Buckley, causing Locklin to stop in fear.

"It's okay, Locklin. It's my friend, Barnabas. He won't hurt you." Buckley's voice held a soothing quality to it that had her looking up at him, searching his face.

"He won't? I don't know him." Locklin looked up at Barnabas. "You're tall."

———

Barnabas grinned at her. "I am. So are all my friends. I'm glad to meet you. Now, how be we find my vehicle and I can take you two home."

"Home? I don't know where I live. Where do I live?" Locklin crawled into the back of Barnabas' truck and shut the door after herself.

"Buckley? What does she mean?" Barnabas' hand on his arm stopped him.

"She can't remember who she is. It must have been the head injury." Buckley stared at the truck door. "What do I do now, Barnabas? We haven't had this before."

"No, I don't think we have. In you go, Buckley. Let's get you home and out of sight." Barnabas nodded at Brady and Ennis as he rounded the front of his truck and jumped up behind the wheel. He turned slightly in his seat to watch Locklin. She's like a lost little lamb, isn't she, Lord? Not knowing who she is or who's after her will be difficult to defend against. And my friend, Buckley, here, Lord, is involved all the way. I know his heart, Lord. He will not walk away from her. And that makes me afraid for him.

Locklin kept her eyes on Buckley, not watching outside the truck. He knew that she was watching him and kept glancing back at her, a smile to reassure her on his face. She finally looked away as Barnabas parked in his designated spot on the Foundation grounds. Her mouth opened at the sight of the three-story building they called home and had their offices in it.

"This is your home, Buckley? It's huge!"

Buckley grinned. "It is. It has apartments on the three floors, offices on the main floor for all of us. There are fifteen of us who live here, including Doc and his Anna. We have security on site as well. This is where the Barnabas Foundation has its offices. Right now, Doc and Anna want you to stay with them."

Locklin took the hand that he extended to her to help her down from the truck, a look of pain on her face as she landed on the ground. He swept an arm around her, leading her into the building, stopping as she did. She stared around the lobby, wonder on her face.

"This is like heaven, Buckley. Are you sure that I'm still alive?" She looked up at him, complete trust in her eyes.

"Not heaven, Locklin. Home. For now. We do need to talk, though. We need to find out what all you remember."

Her brows lowered as she glared at him. "I don't want to remember. That much I know. Whatever it was in my past has terrified me. Can't we leave it there?"

"No, we will deal with it." Barnabas' voice was firm. "Let's get you to Anna."

Anna watched as Buckley walked towards her, unknowing that his heart was on his face as he watched Locklin. She exchanged a glance with Cadee, Benen's wife, who had dropped by, a pile of clothes in her hands. They had been destined for the shelter Cadee's parents ran but Cadee had pulled them from that pile and brought them up at Anna's request.

"I won't stay, Anna. It will be enough for her just to meet you. I'll come back later." Cadee's voice was soft as she moved away. "Call me if you need anything more."

"I will, love. And thank you." Anna's attention went back to Locklin, who stood in front of her, a puzzled look on her face.

"Do I know you?" Locklin's voice was quiet, too quiet Anna thought.

"No, you don't, love. But you will. I understand you met my husband, Doc, earlier."

"I did?" Locklin looked up at Buckley for confirmation.

"You did, Locklin. He's the physician who treated you." He gently nudged her through the door. "In you go. Anna, I suspect that she'll want to clean up. Cadee been around?"

"She has, Buckley. And I have a pile of brand new clothes for Locklin to choose from." Anna's arm was around Locklin, leading her away, not seeing the panicked look the younger woman shot back at Buckley.

"She's got trust issues there, my friend." Barnabas moved into the kitchen, helping himself to the coffee and then pouring a mug for Buckley. "Sit. You're not too steady on your feet yourself."

"No, I'm not. Tomorrow will be worse." Buckley sipped at his coffee, reaching into the cookie tin that sat on the table for one of Anna's cookies. "Where do we go from here, Barnabas?"

—

"I spoke with Will and then John, one of the lawyers. He'll drop around tomorrow. Both suggested that neither one of you say too much today, now that you've given your statements. There will be an investigation into the explosion. Bill said he'd go by the tow yard and pull the GPS and what he needed from your car. That should prove you weren't around her apartment."

"That's good, considering that I have no idea where she lives. Am I a suspect?"

"No. They just need to verify your whereabouts and hers."

"She's a suspect?" Buckley had to tamp down the anger that rose. "He's still trying to control her."

Chapter 5

Staring at the pile of clothes left on the bed for her, Locklin blinked back tears. They are too beautiful for me, she thought, and then wondered why she thought that. She reached out a tentative finger, finally choosing something quickly and rushing through a shower and dressed quickly. She paused to study the bathroom and then the bedroom. One thing that she was sure of, was that she had never had a room like this. Not that she could remember, and right now, she didn't remember a whole lot.

Opening the door quietly, she paused, a prayer rising from her, surprising her. Did she believe in God, she wondered? She must, she felt confident. She stepped into the hallway and saw socked feet in front of her downcast eyes and then felt welcoming arms just sweeping her into a tight hug. Buckley, she thought. He knew when to come and find me.

"You okay?" Buckley's baritone voice, as quiet as he had spoken, swept through her with peace.

"I guess so. I have never had such clothes so. They must have been meant for someone else." Locklin was almost in tears.

"No, they were meant for you. Cadee, a friend's wife and one of the ladies here, collects clothes for the shelter her parents run. She donates them there or to ones who could use them, without any thought of repayment. She has done that for you as a welcome to the family." Buckley turned her to the kitchen, an arm still around her.

"The family? That sounds like a mafia family." Locklin couldn't figure out why Buckley broke out into laughter. "Buckley? What did I say that's so funny?"

"We're a close, God-loving family, Locklin, that just opens up and welcomes the ladies into our midst." He seated her and then paused. "I have no idea what you would like to drink. Or even eat."

"Juice, I think, Buckley. And soup." Anna gave him a hug on the way by, surprising Locklin. "We do that, Locklin. We're huggers in this family. And welcome." Anna was puzzled as Buckley started to laugh once more.

"It's okay, Anna. I said the same thing, and she informed me that it sounded like a mafia family."

Anna laughed even as she bent to hug Locklin. "Far from that, Locklin. And you are indeed a welcome addition to the family."

"But, I'm not. I'm only here for now. I just wish I could remember my past." That distressed her.

"It will come. When you least expect it, you will remember." Doc stood in the doorway, home for the day. "You need to rest and recover, Locklin. That's why you're with us."

Locklin spun, startled, before her eyes closed and she slid for the floor. Buckley was there to catch her, worry on his face as he gathered her to him, and headed

---

after Doc towards her bedroom. Doc shooed him away once he had laid her down.

Buckley paced the kitchen, not sure where he needed to be, pulling out his phone as it vibrated. Brady. Of course, it would be. He stepped out of the apartment to take the call.

"Buckley? Where are you?" Brady's voice was rushed.

"With Doc and Anna. Why?"

"Because I'm on duty and some man was just here looking for you or Locklin. No one helped him out, but it's only a matter of time until someone says something."

"Is that right? Thanks for the heads up, Brady. Stay safe."

"And you. Call if you need any of us. You've been there for us. We'll be there for you. Gotta run." Brady's phone cut off as he answered a call from his partner, Patrick.

Buckley stood in the hallway, back to the wall, head leaning on it, his eyes closed, praying as he didn't think he had ever prayed before. He had never had a lady that had interested him. Not until Locklin. And he had no idea what all that she was involved with. That he would discover over time.

Brandon waited, his eyes searching his friend's face, Burnie at his side. When Buckley finally stirred, they walked towards him.

—

"Buckley?" Brandon's voice had Buckley opening his eyes and peering at him. "You're in pain. You need to be in bed, recovering."

"I can't, Brandon. Not until I find out if Locklin is okay."

"Locklin? Why? Did something else happen?" Burnie stared between Buckley and the closed apartment door.

"She passed out. Doc startled her and she just dropped." Buckley moved towards the apartment door, pausing as Burnie spoke.

"We're praying for you two, Buckley. But you need to heal as well. Staying up, waiting for her to awaken, won't do that."

"I know that, Burnie. I know that. It's just... I just don't know." Buckley's voice died away as he disappeared into the apartment.

Burnie and Brandon shared a look.

"He's got it bad." Brandon grinned. "Now, we get to tease him."

"Not yet." Burnie grinned as well. "That will come. Let his lady heal a bit. I'm going in. Are you?"

Chapter 6

Standing in the lobby the next morning, Locklin looked around, a frown in place. This could not be a business building, she thought. Not with those wonderful seating areas on each side. She moved towards one, a hand out to touch the gas fireplace. This is so nice, she thought. And to think people live in a building like this. Lord, I can't remember what I lived in or how nice or horrible it was. Thank you for letting me see a little bit of heaven on earth before I leave.

She turned as she heard footsteps heading her way and smiled, the smile lighting up her face. Buckley stopped in front of her, his hands reaching for hers.

"You're here. I was just about to head upstairs when I saw you."

"I am. I don't think that I should be." Locklin chewed at her lip.

"Why not? You're part of our family now." Buckley didn't continue, couldn't until he knew more about her. But all he knew was that he was afraid she would just up and disappear and take his heart with her.

"I am?" Locklin looked up at him, a pleased look in her eyes. "I didn't know that. But, you were heading somewhere."

"I was. I was looking for you. I would like to show you around the building. A security guard will go with us when we step outside."

"A security guard? Why?" She stared down at the hand he had extended to her before she took it, liking the feel of his strong grip, and afraid that she would come to like it just a little too much.

"Because someone showed up at the hospital looking for you. No one said where you were. We're just being cautious."

"Oh. I see. But tell me. What is it you do?"

"I'm a minister, pastor, preacher. Whatever it is you want to call me."

"You are? You don't look like one." Locklin studied his face as he grinned down at her. "You're tall."

"I know. Don't hold it against me, okay?"

She shrugged. "Why would I?"

"You're tiny, like Imly. I'll find her at some point and introduce you. I think you two would make good friends."

Locklin finally stood in the rose garden, a hand reaching for an early yellow rosebud. "This is beautiful, Buckley. Someone put a lot of thought into this."

"The Foundation board did. Barnabas' mother, Elizabeth, helped plan the original gardens. The ladies of the family have all had a say in how they have been expanded. Imly runs our vegetable garden, although we all pitch in and help.”

“Where is that? I think I remember having a garden like that at some point.” She took his hand once more as he led her towards the garden. “I can hear waves.”

“You have good hearing. That’s Lake Erie over here. The waves are running high today with the winds on the lake. I’ll take you there once you’re better.”

“You will? I’ll be here that long?” Locklin studied him again, still not sure of what he was saying.

“You will be, Locklin, if I have anything to say about it.” Buckley stared down at her. “The fellows are meeting in a while. Do you have any identification on you?”

“Identification? I don’t know. I have this.” She pulled a small plastic folder from her pocket. “It was in my other jeans. I don’t recognize this person.”

Buckley took it and opened it. “It’s you, Locklin. Somewhat younger and with a different hairstyle. You’re wearing glasses.” Buckley frowned at her. “You really don’t recognize yourself?”

“No. Is that really me?” She leaned against him as she peered down at the driver’s license. “I guess it is. But how do I find out about me? I don’t remember anything at all.” She looked down at her hands. “I’m not wearing rings. So does that mean I am single?”

“I would suspect so.” Buckley swung an arm around her and turned her to the building. “Let’s go in

—

and head for the conference room. It has been used a lot for research in the last couple of years."

"It has? Why?"

"Because ten of my friends here all had what they term as adventures when they met their ladies. Some of the adventures were pretty severe." He held the door to the conference room open for her. "There's only Brandon, Burnie, and Baird here right now. Fellows, this is Locklin."

The men stood, coming to shake her hands, surprising her at how polite they were.

"Do you do that with everyone you meet?" She stared at each one and then down at her hand.

Baird sent Buckley a puzzled look. "We do, Locklin, if I may call you that. It's polite to shake someone's hand when you meet them."

"I know that. It just surprised me. Now, Buckley, how did I know that?"

"Likely because that was how you were raised. Have a seat. We'll start the research. Burnie, here's Locklin's identification, although she says the picture isn't her." He grinned down at her as she frowned.

"You'd say the same if you had lost your memory." She looked around. "There are a lot of computers in here. Why?"

"Because there are fourteen of us who sometimes are in this room. As well as ten other ladies." Baird frowned for a moment. "Do you know how to use a computer?"

Locklin shrugged. "I have no idea. It's like being a newborn and suddenly growing too fast. I have no idea what I do or don't know." She grinned at them. "Is this the adventure that I'm to have?"

Buckley groaned to himself. "I have no idea, Locklin, but it looks as if it's part of it. Here, let me boot up that computer, and then you can see what you do know." He walked away a few moments later, to stand watching her as she studied the keyboard and then the monitor.

"Buckley? What's going on?" Burnie was concerned.

"She's forgotten everything, Burnie. Everything. I don't know how we can keep her safe if we don't know who is after her."

Chapter 7

Buckley finally sat back from his computer and stretched, before rising and heading for the ever-ready coffee pot, refilling his mug and then turning to study the room. Over the course of the morning, Benen and Breck had appeared. Cadee, Berneen, and Imly had been in and introduced themselves to Locklin, finally drawing her away with them. Locklin had looked at Buckley, panic briefly in her gaze before he gave her a smile and nod. She had sighed, he knew, and left with the ladies. He figured that he would need to go find her soon and rescue her.

Breck approached him, a folder in his hand.

"Buckley? What did you get involved in?" His voice was stern.

"I have no idea. All I did was step in to save her from who knows what." Buckley nodded at the folder. "What did you find out?"

"That her father was gunned down in Toronto, coming out of court for testifying against a drug dealer. Her mother had died in childbirth having Locklin. Locklin stayed in her home village, scraping by. The apartment that she had was in a very rundown building that should have been condemned." Breck handed him the folder. "Read this. Come talk to me. And then we'll go talk to Locklin."

Buckley nodded. Then, as Breck turned away, he spoke. "That man? The one that was after her? Did you find any information on him?"

"I did." Breck turned back, concern colouring his face. "He's what we would call the worst guy in the neighbourhood. There have been reports placed with the police about him, but nothing ever has gone to court. The victims, male and female, have either disappeared or retracted their statements."

"That's what she said. That worries me, Breck. How do we help her?"

"For now? We keep her here and safe. I spoke with Will earlier. Dallas will be out. Will wants to start an investigation, but he understands that Locklin's memory is not there."

"I know." Buckley stared at the floor, not quite sure how to phrase his next question.

"She's single, Buckley." Breck smiled in sympathy as he saw Buckley's body sag in relief. "She's single. And very active in her church. That much we have determined. I know the minister through the Foundation. I'll call him and see what else I can find out."

"Please. Let him know that Locklin is safe, and I won't let her come to harm. Not if I can help it." Please, Lord, let her be safe. She's important to me, and I don't want to see her hurt. Not any more. Please, Lord? I've never asked for this before. Never had an interest in a lady. But Locklin is special.

—

Breck watched him walk away, before he turned, shaking his head. He looked up as Brendon approached him, his eyes on Buckley as he walked away.

"Buckley?"

"He's okay. He's in love, but I'm not sure how far he'll take it if Locklin can't remember."

"That's what is worrying us, Breck. We found some more information on her father. It's not looking good for what happened to him." Burnie held up another file. "Here. You take it. I think you'll need to head to see John about this."

"It's that bad?"

"Concerning, shall we say?" Burnie walked away, the door closing behind him.

"It must be concerning for Burnie to react like that." Benen studied the papers in the folder with Breck. "That's her father? I heard of him. Oh, man, what did Buckley get involved in?"

"It wouldn't have mattered to him. He still would have stepped in. It's not in any of you fellows to step away from a lady in trouble." Breck headed out of the conference room, intent of finding Barnabas.

"Barnabas?" Breck tapped at the office door, having cleared his way through past Amy, Barnabas' secretary.

Barnabas looked up, distracted for a moment. "Breck? Just the person I needed to see. Have a seat. Now, about that land we were looking at in town? What is your feeling on that?"

"I like it. It's in a good location and would make a good place for that apartment building. How does the board feel?"

"They feel the same. John's been given the go-ahead to proceed." Barnabas sat back, his eyes on his life-long friend. "But that's not why you're here. You are worried. Buckley?"

"Buckley. I have no idea what he walked into, but Locklin's father was murdered after testifying in a court case. They have never found the assailant yet."

"They haven't?" Barnabas paused. "Logan Dinneen?"

"Logan Dinneen." Breck handed over his folders. "Read these. I have. It's not pretty. This makes it even worse that Locklin can't remember her past. We have no idea who to look for."

Chapter 8

Locklin looked up as Cadee dropped down on the couch in Anna's apartment, holding out a plate of cookies.

"Have one. Anna makes the best cookies and she always has tins full for us. We drop in whenever we want, provided that she hasn't told us not to. She's taken us all in and under her wings." Cadee tilted her head. "You're tired. We've worn you out." She was on her feet, finding a pillow for Locklin's head, making her lie down, covering her with the afghan Anna kept on the couch. "You lie still and sleep if you need to. Do you need your pain medications?"

"Not right now. The headache isn't bad. It's the bruise that hurts." Locklin opened her mouth to protest at Cadee's exclamation before Cadee was away and back with an ice pack wrapped in a soft towel. "You didn't have to do that."

"But I did. You need this. It will help." Cadee tucked her new friend in. "Now, rest. I'll just sit here and watch you sleep." She grinned at Locklin. "And if you feel like it, I'll pray with you."

"Oh, would you? I think that would be nice. I can't remember if I had any friends who did that. You three ladies have been wonderful." Locklin blinked back tears.

"There are seven others who want to meet you as well. They've met this morning already for prayer. If and when you're up to it, we would welcome you to join us."

"I would like that, but I don't think I'll be here that long." She slept, not catching the softened look on Cadee's face.

"You will if Buckley has anything to say. And I think that he will, Locklin. You have his heart. I can see that by how he looks at you and looks after you." She looked up as she felt an arm around her. Benen perched on the side of her chair. "You're here?"

"I am. I just wanted to make sure you didn't need me for anything. I have to run to town. Now, give me a list. What do you want for Locklin?" He bent to kiss his wife.

"You know me too well." Cadee reached into her pocket. "Here. This is the list. If Haleigh and Hollie are around, take them with you. It's been a while since they've been shopping for one of us. They enjoy it so much."

"They already tracked me down and insisted that I needed to take them to town. They have their own list. We'll see how well you've trained them. Love you, sweetheart." With another kiss, he was gone, leaving Cadee smiling at how much she loved her husband.

Locklin had awakened and had watched with interest the interchange between the couple. Cadee caught her movement and looked over at her.

———

"That's my fellow. Benen. He married me when I was out on a mission field, just to make sure I could get out of the country safely. Dad asked him to. We had been friends for years. We had an adventure I'll tell you about sometime, but I will tell you that I almost died from a poisoning. We went through a lot, but we are deeply in love. God has blessed us." She looked around, not seeing anyone else. "Can I tell you a secret that we haven't shared with anyone else?"

Locklin nodded, smiling. "Sure. I think I can keep secrets. You're taking a chance, though."

"You can keep secrets. I know that. I have a good read on people, and I trust you." Cadee paused for a moment. "We're having a baby in about seven months. I think you needed to hear some good news."

"Cadee! That's wonderful. How blessed the little one will be!" Locklin grew sober. "I don't think I'll have married. I'm not the type to."

"Don't sell yourself short, Locklin. I think you will." Cadee looked around as she heard the door and then footsteps heading for the kitchen. "Your fellow is here and I think Breck and Barnabas as well. They always head for the kitchen for coffee and sweets."

"My fellow? Oh, I don't think that I have one of those. I never will." Sadness lingered on Locklin's face as she sat up, wrapping the afghan around herself. Buckley paused before he dropped down beside her, an arm around her to hug her.

Cadee exchanged a look with Breck, who had been watching Locklin intently, and frowned. Something was up. She made to rise, but Breck shook his head. She settled back. Okay, he wants me here. This can't be good.

Locklin looked up at the two other men and then at Cadee.

"You're here. I don't like that. At least, I don't think that I do. You look like you have bad news."

Barnabas and Breck sat, setting down their mugs of coffee and Breck dropping the file folders that he held.

"We do need to talk to you, Locklin. First, may we pray with you? That's how we always start off anything that we are concerned about."

She shrugged, Buckley's arm still around her. "I guess. I have no idea what I do or don't do. And that's frustrating. When will I remember?"

"Likely it will come back over time. Or it may come back all at once. There are some things that you might never remember." Breck nodded at Buckley, who led them off in prayer. When they were finished, Breck studied his hands, not quite sure how to begin. He finally looked up at Locklin, to find her watching him.

"You need to talk to me?" Locklin looked between the three men. "I don't like those looks. At least, I don't think I do."

"We have news, Locklin. We have been researching you, as I am sure Buckley has explained." Breck paused, his eyes on Buckley.

"I did, Breck. Go on. What do you need to say to Locklin?"

"Locklin, we have determined something about your family. I'm sorry, but your mother died in childbirth with you. Your father raised you, up until about a year ago. At that point, he had been testifying in a drug trial. He was not one of the parties that were arrested. He just happened to have information that helped to arrest them." Breck paused, not quite sure how to continue.

"And he was killed? Is that what you don't know how to tell me?" Locklin blinked, not quite sure how to react. "I'm guessing that I grieved. I would if he had been my father. But I don't remember him. And that sucks. Big time."

Chapter 9

Breck nodded before looking over at Barnabas, finding his gaze intent on Locklin. He sighed to himself. This was not going the way that they had prayed. They had prayed that this would trigger a memory for Locklin, and it hadn't.

"Breck, do you have a photo of her father? That might help." Cadee spoke from where she had moved to sit beside Locklin, reaching for one of the other lady's hands.

"I do. Locklin, we are so sorry for you. We cannot imagine how difficult this is for you, to be here with strangers, not remembering who you are or your past. Or even why you were on the run." Barnabas handed Buckley the photo. "This is the one that we found. Your father was a hard worker, not making a lot, but enough to keep you two from want. He made sure that you were taken care of. Breck has spoken with the minister in your town. He was very concerned about you. He warned Breck that you should not ever come back there."

Locklin blinked. "But it's my home. I need to go there." Her voice wobbled. "I have nowhere else."

"But you do, Locklin. You have us. We can become your family if you let us." Buckley hugged her tighter, his chin resting on her head. "None of us want you to walk away and into danger."

Locklin had turned to study Buckley, not sure what he was saying. She frowned for a moment.

"I'm not sure that I should. If I am a danger to you, I should leave." She started to rise but found Buckley had tightened his arm around her.

"Locklin, I am about to say something that we should really discuss in private. But I know these friends of mine. I know that they will support me in what I say." He paused, biting at his lip. "I would like to offer you my name in marriage, to have you become my bride."

"You can't do that!" Locklin was shocked. "You can't!" She whispered it again, her eyes on him. "You don't know me. I could be a criminal, setting you up for something."

Buckley laid a finger over her lips, stilling her words. "I see the real you, Locklin. You are not a criminal. You don't have it in you. Just think about what I asked, and pray about it." He shared a look with Cadee, who nodded. "Talk to some of the ladies here. Berneen, Cadee, Imly, for some. They married quickly in order to protect themselves. Berneen married Baird to save his life. I would offer you my home and my name." He dropped his gaze, not wanting to see the rejection in her eyes that he was sure he would see.

Breck and Barnabas shared a look. They had felt this was the step that Buckley would likely take. John had been around, taking the identification that he offered and heading into the court, to obtain the necessary licenses. None of them knew when Buckley would make the offer, but they knew him. They knew that he would not let a lady like Locklin walk out of his life, not if he could possibly help it.

Locklin studied the photo of her father, a finger tracing the face. He should be familiar to me, Lord, but he isn't. I just don't know why. I am so scared and again I don't know why. Buckley is offering to put his life on the line for me. Do I accept or do I walk away, running for my life, not knowing when it will end? Please, dear Lord, I need an answer and a peace that very answer. I need to learn to pray as I have never prayed before.

Buckley sighed to himself. He had blown it, he thought. In his eagerness to protect her, he had blown what chance he had with her. He rubbed at his forehead, his headache worsening. He refused to look at Breck or Barnabas, not wanting to see pity on their faces, yet knowing they would never show that to him. All they would show would be their support of him.

"Buckley?" Locklin's voice was low. "Did you mean that?"

"Mean what? That I would marry you? Absolutely." He watched as she glanced at the other three in the room, reading their thoughts and then lifting her eyes to where Anna and Doc stood, their acceptance of her on their faces.

"Then, I guess, I accept." She buried her face in her hands. "That's not how I should say that. Thank you, Buckley. I will marry you."

Buckley simply reached to hug her, his cheek on her hair. He blinked rapidly, not sure what had just happened, but realized that he had taken the step so

—

many of his friends had taken. He was sure that it was right. God had given him peace about it.

Breck sighed to himself. He had done it, hadn't he, Lord? Put himself out there as a target, just to protect a lady. Barnabas shook his head at Cadee who rose and walked softly from the room, linking her arm with Anna. Doc sat beside Locklin, waiting for her to look around.

"Locklin? Let me take the place of your father for just a moment? You are sure?" At her nod, Doc continued. "Then, let us arrange it for you. Breck told me that one of the Foundation lawyers had taken both of your identification and headed in to get the license. I spoke with the minister, Jack, who is taking Buckley's place while he is on vacation. He will marry you."

Barnabas spoke in turn. "I have talked to Will, Buckley. He suspected that you would take this step. He knows you fellows too well. He suggested that you not wait for too long. That if you married, she would have your protection but also the protection of the Foundation and its lawyers as well as the protection and support of the police in town."

"That's true." Buckley looked down at Locklin. "I won't rush her. Not at all."

Locklin looked up. "Buckley, do we need to marry right away? I mean, like today. I'm not ready. I don't have a dress to wear." Tears sparkled on her lashes.

"I don't care about that, Locklin. All I care about is keeping you safe." Buckley looked up as Anna cleared her throat. "Here, go with Anna. She'll find something for you to wear. If you are willing, would you marry me today?"

Locklin looked at Anna and then back at Buckley, nodded, unable to speak. Buckley hugged her once more, stood, and drew her with him to Anna, who simply wrapped them both in a hug and prayed for them.

Chapter 10

Late that night, Buckley wandered his apartment, coffee mug in hand, not sure if he had made the right decision. He felt that he had. He had prayed hard and long and had not felt God stopping him. His friends had prayed with him as they gathered in the chapel, each one knowing that Buckley would not have taken the step if he had not felt it was the right one. They also knew that he would walk away from his beloved church and congregation if he had to, to protect everyone.

He paused at the bedroom that Locklin had chosen, resting his hand flat on the door, his heart raised in prayer for his Locklin, his bride. Mom and Dad, you would love her. I know that you would. I just wish that you were here to meet her. I never knew that day, when I was only a young teen, you left for that mission trip, and that cyclone hit the village you were in, wiping it out and taking everyone with it. I miss you both. Buckley wiped at the tears on his face. His parents had supported him in all his decisions, talking through them with him, and then praying with him. He needed their prayers right now and then felt peace. He remembered the passage in John, where Christ had prayed for those who were His, all those years ago.

Locklin raised her head, hearing Buckley's footsteps pause for a moment and then walk on by. She snuggled down under the covers, for the first time that she felt she could remember being warm with enough blankets. She felt the sheet, the soft flannel comforting. She slept, her heart raised in prayer and thankfulness, her earnest plea that God would teach her how to pray, to support her husband. She knew that she would need it, being a minister's wife, and not having her memory. She slept, not knowing that the next weeks would test both her faith and Buckley's and test the marriage that they had entered into with God's blessing.

Early the next morning, Locklin crept from her bed, dressed, and then wandered the apartment on her own. Buckley had given her a tour the night before, but her head had been aching too much to take in her new home. She stood in his office, a hand on his chair, praying for him, not quite sure what her duties would be. She ran her hands along the volumes of books on the floor to ceiling bookshelves, finding to her delight the classic novels that she had always wanted to read but had no time to do that.

Locklin searched the kitchen, finding it well stocked with food. She stood staring at some of the small appliances, not quite sure what some of them were before she reached for the eggs and bread in the fridge, and then the ham and fresh peppers and onions. She searched and found the cheese. She would make an omelet for breakfast, she thought, finding the skillet that she needed. Humming, Locklin worked away, content to be in such a beautiful kitchen, she thought,

Buckley stood and watched her, a sigh rising from him. He had had a call from Breck, warning him that the man who had been searching for Locklin had tracked her to the Foundation building. Security had stopped him from entering the main gate late the night

---

before. He had become violent with them and they had called in reinforcements. Breck suspected that he would be back as soon as he could. They needed to talk to Locklin again.

Locklin looked around, a smile brightening her face, before she frowned as she looked down at the breakfast that she had prepared. She had searched for the dishes in the cupboard, delighting in matched dishes, not quite sure why.

"I'm sorry. I should have waited to find out what you wanted to eat." She rubbed her hands together nervously.

"Whatever you have prepared is what I want." Buckley grasped her hands, stilling their movement before he raised them to kiss them. "Now, let's get you sitting, and we can eat." He sat beside her, a hand reaching for hers as he asked the blessing on the food.

He finally sat back, his eyes on her, even as he prayed for her. He knew Breck would be around and he suspects Brody would be as well, in his paralegal work mode.

Locklin tilted her head, watching him as well. "Buckley? You're troubled. I'm sorry. I didn't mean to make you marry me. I can leave."

"No, it's not that, Locklin love. I will follow you wherever you go if you do ever leave me. It's not that. Breck called earlier. The man from the hospital has tracked you to here. He was prevented from entering the premises last night and arrested, but we suspect that he will return."

"Do you have a picture of him? Maybe I would remember why he's after me." Locklin twisted the china cup that Buckley had found for her tea, simply telling her that it had been his mother's and she would want her to use it.

"Breck likely will. Another friend, Bradon, will be with him. He's a paralegal and wants to draw up some legal paperwork for us."

"Such as?" Locklin was puzzled. She didn't think that she needed any legal paperwork.

"For starters, power of attorneys for us, medical and finance. He also wants to do a preliminary will for us. We can always change it as we need to."

"Oh, I see. To protect us? Is that why?"

"Exactly. He went through some hard stuff with his wife, Ker, regarding her parents' estates. Their story is quite the tale. I'll walk you through them all later today. That way, you'll have an understanding of what happened with each one."

"How many of you are there?"

"With Barnabas, there are fourteen of us. Eleven of us are now married. We also need to talk about finances. I am paid through the Foundation, which they do with all of us fellows. That allows our employers to hire on someone else without worrying about money. It's part of being encouragers, as Barnabas was to Paul." Locklin's gaze never left his face. "Even as a minister of the local church, my wages are paid. That has allowed the church to reach out to the community and help where needed." Buckley paused. "As part of

—

their practice of being encouragers, and to help the couples, the Foundation board agreed that the wives would receive a wage through the Foundation as well. That allows them to either work in the community, volunteer, return to school, or just be at home."

"They do that?" Locklin's voice was quiet. "I never knew that people did that nowadays. I think that it's wonderful. But I don't qualify."

"But you see, you do. You're my wife. Breck or Barnabas will talk to you about it later on. But for now, you're here, with me. I am so glad that you are. I think that I've been waiting forever for you." His last words were barely audible.

Locklin studied him, not sure if she had heard him right, or that she had heard him right when he had called her love. It made her happy but she had to remember her history. She might not be the right one for him. And that saddened her.

Chapter 11

Locklin turned from where she had been standing at the door of the office, looking out over the grounds. She smiled tentatively at Breck and then at the man with him.

"Locklin. This is Brody. He's here for what we discussed." Buckley's arm around her drew her to a seat on the couch. "I know Breck. He wants to pray first."

"He does? Okay." Locklin smiled at Breck and then bowed her head.

Breck handed over a folder to Buckley. "In this is a photo of the man who tried to break through our defenses last night. He didn't make it. Take a look at it. Tell me if you think you know him."

Buckley opened the folder, peering closely at the photo. "This is not the man who I stopped from harming Locklin. I've never seen him before."

Locklin leaned against him. "I don't know him. I wouldn't, now would I?"

"We were hoping that it might trigger a memory." Breck nodded. "It was a long shot. He's a known associate of the drug dealers whom your father was testifying against. We're not sure why they are looking for you."

"I don't know that either." Locklin paused and then shook her head. "I'm sorry. I can't remember. I keep saying that. It's not right. I should be able to." She rubbed at the receding lump on her head.

"That's okay, Locklin. He's still in jail. He couldn't make his bail. He's also wanted in other areas. He'll be transferred there today." Breck hesitated and then spoke quietly. "We need both of you to be ever so careful. Buckley, you understand, having been part of what the others went through. Locklin, trust what Buckley tells you. I know it will be difficult for you at times. Talk to the other ladies. Hear their stories. That will help."

"You're scaring me, Breck." Locklin's eyes were huge with fright.

"I don't mean to, Locklin. I just want to warn you to be very careful. Even here on the Foundation grounds. Now, I'm off to a meeting that I can't miss. We'll talk again." Breck was gone before either one of the couple could say anything.

"Did he really just do that?" Locklin frowned as she strained to see through the doorway.

Buckley and Brody laughed.

"He did, love. He did." Buckley grinned at the frown she directed his way. "He'll be back. Trust me on that."

"That's what I'm afraid of. He'll be back with more photos of men that I don't know." She glared at the two men as they continued to laugh. "Now, he's here for a reason. What is it?" She pointed at Brody.

Brody laughed. "You got me there, Locklin. Buckley asked me to stop by. I was going to anyway. We need to do some legal stuff for you."

"Legal stuff? How definitive and descriptive. Is that what you call it to your clients?" Locklin was tired and although she didn't know it, when she grew tired, she could become combative to an extent.

"Legal paperwork, then. First, we need to look at the powers of attorney. Financial. Medical. Particularly medical. We'll make sure that the hospital is aware of this, Buckley. We'll also need to let your family physician know. I assume that Locklin will become one of his patients?"

"I would assume so. I'll talk to him on Monday. Now, about the wills?"

"Wills as well. Locklin, I know you can't remember, but have you ever thought about a will?"

"You just told me that I couldn't remember that." Locklin was puzzled, not sure if she ever had. "I'm not sure that I ever did. From what I have been told, I didn't have anything of value." She blinked rapidly to dispel the tears that had gathered.

"I'm sorry, Locklin. I didn't mean to upset you." Brody was concerned about her. "How are you feeling?"

"Feeling? Me? How would you expect me to feel? Apparently, I was chased, jumped in a car, run off the road, and ended up slammed against a tree. Then I'm dragged here, dropped into a huge family that's not a family, and then married. How am I to

—

feel?" She looked sheepishly, her eyes on Buckley as she finished. "I'm sorry. That wasn't nice of me."

"But it's true, Locklin. It's all true. I'm sorry that it had to happen to you. But I'm not sorry I was the one who rescued you. Now, Brody, what do we have to do?"

"Let me have a few moments. I can do the documents up right away, have you proof them, and then print them. You can sign them. I'll need some witnesses but I know Baird and Berneen are around as are some of the others."

"It doesn't matter, other than for Ker. She shouldn't be the one as a witness."

"No, she shouldn't. Let's get this done and then I'll be gone." He looked up, hesitating for a moment. "Ker asked if you two would like to come for dinner. It's up to you. She just wanted to extend the invitation."

Buckley kept his eyes on Locklin, even as her body sagged against his, fatigue and pain drawing her strength from her.

"Let's see what this afternoon brings."

"That's fair. Now, here. Sign here and here. Berneen and Baird, you two need to sign. Thanks for coming on short notice."

"Not a problem." Baird spoke for both Berneen and himself. "Buckley has gone above and beyond for us all. We have felt his prayers in whatever it was that we have faced, and in the solutions we have found. It's our turn to be there for him."

—

Chapter 12

A week later, Locklin wandered once more in the lobby, the security guard on duty keeping an eye on her. She had become accustomed to that, and to having someone shadow her if she stepped outside. She had wandered the gardens, checked out the gym, looked over Hagen's shop, and been to the lake with Buckley, just as he promised. She was starting to feel better physically, but emotionally she was on a roller coaster ride, she thought.

Hearing her name called, she turned, finding Imly running towards her. It never failed to amaze her how much energy Imly had tucked into her petite frame.

"Locklin! I was hoping to find you here. I'm having a tea party and I want you to come." Imly linked her arm with Locklin's.

"You are? And why me?"

"And why not you? Come on. We have all the ladies together for a change. Hailey and Hollie are there. So is Anna and her sister, Amy, who is secretary to Barnabas."

"That sounds like quite a crowd. You don't need me." Locklin hesitated just inside Imly's apartment door.

—

"Oh, but we do." Fynn appeared, reaching to hug Locklin and then draw her into the living room. "We have a special seat of honour just for you."

"You do? You shouldn't." Locklin looked around. "Wait a moment. This is more than just a tea party. I see all sorts of goodies."

"It is a tea party." Ennis spoke up. "It's also a shower for you. We wanted to do something to welcome you to the family. This is our way of doing it. In fact, you're the first one that we've done this for. So it is very special."

"Buckley is special to all of us. He'll tease and torment us, but he loves us all. He is such an example to us, even when he is struggling. God chose you as his helpmeet. That makes you special." Guenivere spoke for the group. "Please, Locklin?"

Locklin searched each of the ladies' faces, finding acceptance and not condemnation in them.

"What can I say but thank you?" She blinked back tears even as Cadee hugged her.

"Then, let's party!" The women laughed at Hollie's comment.

Later that afternoon, Imly and Cadee helped Locklin gather her goodies, as the twins called them, and head for her own apartment. She had been shocked and then surprised at the thoughtful gifts that she had been given. Locklin hugged the two ladies as they left before she headed for her own bedroom, staring down at the gifts. A nice sweater or two, a gold cross from one of the couples, bath stuff that she had no idea even existed. Some nice enlarged photos. A leather diary. A Bible that she reached for, realizing that her own was likely gone in the fire. She blinked back tears as she then reached for the china teapot and cups and saucers that the twins and Berneen's brother, Darbie, had given her, and turned for the kitchen, standing for a moment just staring around.

Buckley found her still standing there when he came in. He hesitated for a moment to watch her, finding his heart opening up more and more to her. A fervent prayer was raised for her, that she would remember who she was. He had met with the church board that afternoon and had been given their blessings on his marriage, and just when did they get to meet his wife, anyway? That had been arranged for that evening, a light supper at the church with the members and their spouses.

Locklin jumped as she felt arms come around her and then she leaned back against Buckley. I could grow to like this a lot, she thought.

"Have a good day, love?" Buckley's voice was low in her ears.

"I did. The ladies gave me a shower. They said it was the first one for anyone here."

"And it is. They're a wonderful group. I'm glad you're part of them."

Locklin twisted in his arms. "They shouldn't have, but it was nice. I got to meet everyone, I think, other than Ennis' cousin's wife and Fynn's sister-in-law."

—

"Alice would have been on duty. She's a police officer. And Eric and his wife are away on vacation." His finger touched the teapot. "This is nice."

"The twins and Darbie picked it out. I think I like tea, but I'm just not sure about anything." She looked up at him. "You're quiet."

"I am. I had a meeting with the church board this afternoon."

"Oh no! They fired you!" Locklin was horrified at the thought. "It's all my fault." She struggled to free herself from him.

Buckley simply hugged her tighter. "On the contrary, I was given congratulations and asked when we could meet them. They would like to do a light supper this evening. If you're up to it."

She frowned at him, earning herself another grin. "I guess. I'm not sure, Buckley. I know nothing about being a minister's wife. And there's that danger hanging over me. What if it hits the church?"

Chapter 13

Looking around, the man snuck into the garden area of the Foundation grounds, watching for Locklin. He knew that she was here. He had seen her. His boss wanted her. The man had no idea why, but there had been enough rumours and gossips among the employees for him to fear for her life.

He looked around and grimaced. She wasn't here. She was always out here at this time of day. He couldn't hang around or else he would be caught. A sound behind him had him stopping in his backward trek.

"All right, my friend. We're heading into the building." Bradon stood there, Kade, his dog beside him. "You're not part of the family. In you go."

The man sighed. He had blown it. Now, his life would be forfeit, that much he knew. Unless he could swing a deal and leave.

Bradon studied the man closely. He was neat and well kept. Just why he was on the grounds, he would leave that for the authorities to determine. He looked around as Baird and Blair approached him.

"Where'd you find him?" Baird nodded towards the man.

"In the rose garden. I suspect that he was looking for Locklin. She's usually out there at this time of day." Bradon looked the man over again.

"Not today. I met Buckley earlier. They were heading out somewhere for a while." Baird kept quiet where they were heading.

"I see." Bradon looked around as he heard a car door shut. "Here's your ride, my friend. My advice to you is to own up to why you're here. It will go easier with you if you do."

Buckley watched from where he stood near his car, Locklin peering out his open door.

"Who's that?"

"I have no idea, love, but I suspect that he was after you." Buckley slipped behind the wheel. "Right now, we're heading for the church. You need to become familiar with where I work."

She studied him. "Are you sure that you're a minister? You don't act like one."

Buckley laughed at her comment. "I am. I have the diplomas to prove that. But I know what you're saying."

"You do?" Locklin rubbed at her temple. "Buckley, will I ever remember?"

"I am sure that you will. Sometimes it takes great fear or sudden shock to do that."

"That's what I am afraid of. They'll try to do something to you, I'll remember, and then you'll walk out of my life."

"Never, love. I would never do that." Buckley pulled to a stop in the church lot and came around to help her from the car, holding tight to her quivering hand. "I will never leave you."

Late that afternoon, Dallas stood in the sanctuary, his eyes closed, feeling peace flowing through him. He always did when he was there. He felt closer to God when he was in church, and knew that was true but he needed it today, more than any other day. His eyes opened to find Locklin standing in front of him, a hymn book in her hands, a puzzled look on her face.

"Dallas?"

"I'm okay, Locklin." Dallas grinned at her. "I'm okay. I just needed to take a moment and commune with God. And how are you this fine day?"

She frowned at him. "I have no idea how I am to be. What news do you have?"

"I like you. Direct and to the point." He pointed to the front pew. "Can we sit? I was hoping to talk with you."

"Sure. Whatever." Locklin shrugged. "Buckley is on a conference call, I think. He should be done soon."

"We can wait for him if you wish." Dallas sighed as he stretched out his legs. "It's been a long day."

"Has it? And you're here, trying to talk to me." She looked around. "Go ahead. We can always catch Buckley up on what we talked about." Locklin jumped as she felt Buckley sit beside her. "You're here?"

———

"I am. The call was just finishing when I heard Dallas. Dallas?" Buckley looked over Locklin's head at him.

"Buckley. Locklin. I have news. And I am not sure how to express it." Dallas looked puzzled and then sad.

"And why is that?" Locklin studied him. "Is it that bad?"

"Not necessarily. But it does relate to what happened to you." He pulled a photo from a folder and handed it to her. "I know you may not recognize this woman. But can you please just take a look at it?"

Locklin took it, staring down at it, Buckley's arm around her as he stared at it as well.

"It looks like you, love. Dallas?"

Dallas simply shook his head, his eyes on Locklin.

"Locklin?"

Locklin looked up, a frown on her face. "I'm sorry, Dallas. I don't know this person. I mean, she looks like me, but I'm sorry."

"That's okay, Locklin." Dallas shared a look with Buckley. "I can tell you who she is. That might trigger a memory. She is your mother's sister. She died about six months ago. She had tried to find you but couldn't. She even went to your home area and was sent away."

"She did?" Locklin looked shocked. "Oh, I wish I had known. I would have loved to have met family."

Chapter 14

Locklin searched for Buckley that evening, not finding him in the apartment. She paused, frowning, before she grabbed her keys and headed for the chapel. Not here, she thought, before she turned in a circle, not sure where to go.

Burnie was watching her and then approached, finding her staring at him.

"Locklin? Can I help you?"

"You can. Do you know where Buckley is?"

"Sure. He's in the chapel. Have you searched there?"

"I did. He wasn't there. Where is the conference room that you all talk about?"

Burnie motioned with his hand. "This way. I'm heading there. How are you feeling now?"

She shrugged. "Physically I am better. It's just this memory loss that I am having trouble dealing with." She stood in the conference room, staring around. "This is a conference room? It looks more like you would see in a police story, where they all try and solve their crimes."

Burnie grinned. "That's what we do here." He looked around. "No, Buckley isn't here. How be I show you around and you can get a taste of what we do?"

"Sure, why not? Maybe it will trigger something with me. But I'm not holding my breath waiting for that. I'd be too blue in the face if I did." She walked away, not hearing Burnie's soft laughter at her expression.

Buckley paused as he entered, surprised to see Locklin there and deep in conversation with Brady. He turned as Burnie approached.

"She was looking for you, Buckley. I found her outside the chapel, looking lost and forlorn."

"She was? I thought I had told her where I was going. I guess I forgot." Buckley rubbed at his cheek. "I need to do better."

"It will come, Buckley. At least she didn't go outside looking for you."

"No, that's something to be thankful for. How'd she end up in here?"

"I brought her. She asked where the room was. She's been going around, watching everything, talking to the fellows. She asks some tough and discerning questions."

"I would think that she does. She's a thinker." Buckley excused himself and moved towards Locklin, finding her looking up as she heard his steps.

"Buckley? You're here. Brady has been explaining this program to me. It's fascinating. I never knew you could find out ancestors and all that so easily." She beamed at him, drawing him into her beauty.

"We can. Has he been searching for you?"

"He has. Brady, did you say that you could print this?"

"I can. I can also send a link to Buckley and he can pull it up on his personal computer for you."

"Oh! He can?" She sat back, frowning at him, causing him to grin at her. "Stop smirking. I didn't know that. Or at least, I don't think that I did. Maybe?"

"You sound definite there, love. How be we print it, take it home, and then go over it? Brady will continue to add and we can find what he's adding as we work through it."

Locklin was on her feet, already moving towards the printer. Not seeing the papers coming out, she spun and stomped back to stand by Brady. "Okay, buster. Where is it?"

Brady was laughing as he pointed to the printer. "Right there. You hadn't given me time to print it."

Buckley bit back his own laughter, not wanting Locklin to think he was laughing at her. She frowned at him as well before spinning and heading for the printer. Her exclamation that there were too many pages had the fellows laughing quietly.

Brady watched as the couple left before he began to laugh harder. "When she recovers her memory, she'll give Buckley a hard time."

"Yeah. She's just right for him." Burnie turned back, a smirk on his face. "He deserves that. Now, where do we stand? And how far have we researched Locklin?"

"About as far as we can. I put in a call to Emma. She's to get back to me." Brendon looked up. "Any word on that fellow who was here today?"

"Not that I have heard. Dallas hasn't been in contact today." Brennen sent off a text. "He'll get to us when he can with what he can."

Buckley set the papers on the kitchen table and then just swept Locklin into a hug. She surprised him by hugging him back before she leaned to one side and looked up at him.

"Where do we start, Buckley? How do we find out who I am?"

"With what we've been doing. Dallas called. The fellow that they found here? He's an undercover officer, apparently. He can't say more than that."

"Oh. Well, okay. I guess that's all right." Locklin moved away, reaching for her new teapot. "Do you want some tea, Buckley?"

"Yes, that would be nice." He grinned at her. "You just want to use your new teapot."

"Well, there's that." She turned, watching him intently. "Buckley, aren't we supposed to be getting packages with photos crossed off in them, death threats, horrible text messages, and emails, being stalked? Is that happening?"

"Not that I am aware of. We would have been told. I hope it never happens."

"But it will. I just know it." She paced to the end of the counter and back. "I don't want a phone, Buckley, but I know I need one."

"You do. I have one here for you. The only ones with the number other than myself are the family here, and Dallas and Will. We're trying to keep it as private as we can." He handed it to her. "We've programmed in all the numbers for you."

"You have? You're so thoughtful, Buckley." Locklin peered up at him, finding that look in his eyes again. "How did you ever not marry before?"

"I was waiting for you." He watched as she blushed before he ran the back of his hand down her cheek. "I was simply waiting for you."

Chapter 15

Locklin let out a scream as she opened the package, dropping it to the floor and falling herself, to scramble backward. She drew up her knees, wrapping her arms around them, and hiding her face. Buckley slid to a halt, running towards her as he heard the scream. He stared at the package before he was on his knees, fighting her to wrap her in his arms and then draw her up and away from the hallway.

"Locklin? Talk to me. Locklin?" His frantic words finally reached to her and she threw her arms around him. "Locklin?"

"That package. Get it out of here, Buckley. Please?" Her sobs shook her frame, distressing him.

Buckley reached for his phone, called Dallas, and demanding that he send someone. That there was a package that Locklin had opened and that it had frightened her soundly.

An hour later, Buckley still sat in his chair, Locklin tight in his arms, her head buried against him. She had finally stopped shaking but her face was still white, the shock of what she had seen running deep within her.

Dallas watched her before he looked at Buckley, finding his attention on his wife. He sat, waiting until Buckley looked up.

"Dallas?" Buckley's voice was shaken.

"It's gone, Buckley. Did you see what it was?"

"No. All I heard was Locklin scream. She had gone down for the mail, something she will do if I'm on the phone or deep in my studies. That's what she had done today. The mail is on the table, I think. She had opened the box, I guess, and that's when I heard her scream. What was in it?"

"A blood-covered teddy bear. It shook the crime scene techs as well. There may be a note in it, but we'll have to wait to see what they find." Dallas looked at Locklin. "Locklin? Can you talk with me?"

She shook her head, her eyes turning to watch him. "I can't. I don't even want to think about that thing, whatever it was." She burrowed closer to Buckley. "Buckley, make them stop, please? Make them stop? They keep doing this to me. Sending me boxes with stuff in it. I don't want them anymore. Please make them stop?" Her sobs shook her once more.

Buckley could feel anger growing in him and knew that he needed to address it.

"Dallas, who?"

"That's what we'll work on. There was no return address on the box. In fact, it really doesn't look as if it came through the mail. I'm waiting to speak with the security people who were on duty today and to pull the security feed from today."

"Find them. That's all I ask. I won't have her troubled like this." Buckley bit down his words. "I know. You can't help it. And that you can't stop it."

—

Buckley tightened his arms around Locklin. "Maybe we need to go away somewhere."

"That won't work, Buckley. They'd just follow you. You'd be out there on your own. Here, you have your friends. You have us. You need that."

Buckley finally nodded, his eyes moving past Dallas to find Breck and Doc there. Dallas had sent for them. Doc moved towards them, setting his bag down on the table.

"Buckley?"

"She's terrified, Doc. She had only stopped shaking and then she remembered getting packages like this one. That started it all over again." Buckley looked devastated. "I think she is starting to remember things. This is not what I wanted. Not these things."

"We can't pick and chose what she remembers. Locklin?" Doc waited patiently until she looked at him, drawing in a breath at the haunted, hollow look in her eyes. "Can I listen to your heart, Locklin? Buckley can still hold you."

Locklin finally nodded, submitting to Doc's examination, but not moving a fraction of an inch from Buckley's firm hug. She settled back against him, her eyes shifting between the four men, listening to their quiet conversation.

Dallas finally spoke. "Locklin? I think that you remembered something. You told Buckley that you had had packages like these before. Is that correct?"

Shrugging, Locklin refused to answer before Buckley spoke.

"Locklin? We're trying to help you. Do you remember anything?"

She nodded at last and then spoke, her voice so low that the men had to strain to hear it.

"I think so. I can remember seeing something like that bear and the blood before. More than once. I just don't remember when or where." She looked up at him, her face pale and wan, her eyes dark with her fear. "I don't remember when. But I have seen them."

"Okay. That's okay, Locklin." Dallas had been watching her. "Did you tell anyone?"

She shrugged. "I don't know. I'm sorry. I don't know." Her eyes closed and she slept, unaware of the concern on the faces of all the men.

"Doc? What happens now?" Buckley finally asked the question that he had been hesitant to.

"We wait, Buckley. This may trigger her memory, or again, it might not. Time is all we have right now."

"And time may not be enough. They have followed her to here, Buckley. Somehow, they made you and followed you." Dallas stared at his friend before he spoke again. "And that makes you a target as well. You know that from the others. They'll go after you to get to her."

"As long as they leave the church and the people alone, they can come after me." Buckley shook his head. "But that's what they'll do. They'll go after them to get to me."

"The board is aware of that, Buckley. I spoke with the chairman earlier. They want no changes. The board will go to the people on Sunday, explain what is going on, and give the people the option of coming or not. We already live stream the service." Breck stopped, his mind working. "They need you there, Buckley, no matter how hard it is. They need to see you and to see Locklin."

Chapter 16

Buckley paced the apartment that night, stifling a yawn. He had finally gotten Locklin settled for the night, not without a great deal of difficulty. She had simply refused to let him out of her sight, and that troubled him. How was he to do his visits to the sick and shut-ins, to the ones hospitalized, keep up with his meetings and studies at the church, if he couldn't leave her? He prayed as he had never prayed before, finding the experience that they were going through driving him deeper and deeper into prayer and into a study about it. His favourite passage in John came to mind. He loved that he had been prayed for in the garden all those hundreds of years ago.

He turned finally, not sure where to go or what to do. Buckley reached for his phone as it chimed, studying the number and sighed. Charles Turner, the board chair, was calling.

"Buckley? You've been on my mind tonight. How are you and your beautiful wife?"

"To tell the truth, Charles? I'm not sure. We had a disturbing incident today, and it frightened Locklin badly."

"Is that right? This morning, you say? I had an urge to pray for you. Listen? Can we meet? Your place, tomorrow, if I can? No, nothing serious. I just need to pray in person with you both."

"Charles, thank you. I am needing that. In fact, I am not sure with what is happening with us how safe the church and people with be with me around."

"We have talked it over as a congregation. We are standing behind you all the way. We'll talk tomorrow. No rash decisions, young man. You came in when we needed an interim, Barnabas finding you in your home province and bringing you here, without any thought that you would be needed so quickly. You are dear to our hearts, son. We'll talk."

Buckley set his phone down, and then cradled his head on his folded arms, his shoulders shaking as he wept. It was something that he did infrequently, but having spent the last year or more fighting to save his friends and their ladies and now facing the unknown with Locklin, he had reached his limit. He didn't hear Locklin as she rose and searched for him, standing for a moment in the office doorway, watching him before she was across the room, her arms around him, her tears wetting his shirt before he simply reached and swept her into his arms, their cheeks touching, their tears mingling.

Locklin finally drew back, her hand on his cheek, her eyes watchful.

"Buckley?" Her voice held the question that she refused to ask.

"Locklin, I love you. I never dreamt that I would have such a beautiful lady in my life. I am so afraid that I will lose you."

She nodded. "I'm scared too, Buckley, that whoever this is will get to you." She tilted her head to watch him. "We've never talked about your family."

"I lost them to a cyclone overseas. They were on a short-term mission trip. I had just about finished seminary when Barnabas tracked me down and offered me a position, paid for by the Foundation. We were working out the details when they needed an interim pastor here. And I took it on and then the church took me on. Mom and Dad would love this church. I miss them so much at times."

Locklin hugged him, her head on his shoulder. "Sometimes that can overwhelm a person. I wish I could remember mine, but it's only bits and pieces that I remember. Not enough to get a picture. It's frustrating." She was silent for a while, content just to be with him. "Something has me puzzled."

"And that would be?"

"You fellows all have the same initials. Is there a reason for that?"

Buckley gave a quick grin. "There is. God was specific with Barnabas. Everyone he hired had to be an orphan and share his initials. He was true to that command. We have been blessed with him as our employer, Breck as his second in command. The fellows are all great friends, and they are blessed with their ladies."

"I see. That's interesting. And I see that each of the ladies' names start with a different letter of the alphabet in order, except it started with the letter B."

"It does. We've talked about that. We figure Barnabas' lady's name with start with the letter A."

"Does he have a lady?"

"That we don't know. He's never said." Buckley paused. "He can be a very private person. I suspect there was someone in his past."

Locklin nodded. "Yes, he is like that." She looked around. "Did I hear your phone?"

"You did. It was Charles. He wants to meet with us tomorrow." His finger laid across her lips to still her protest. "He wants to pray with us. We have the support of the church family."

"But what if I bring harm to them? What then?" Locklin had to admit to herself that she was terrified of doing just that.

"We'll deal with what we have to." Buckley studied her, finding her not looking at him. "When you said you had received packages like that before, do you remember anything else?"

"I said that?" At his nod, she frowned, a puzzled look on her face. "I don't remember that at all, Buckley. I really don't. I was terrified this morning."

"We know you were. I was scared for you, love." He set her on her feet and rose. "How be you head back to bed? You need to rest."

"That's what everyone keeps telling me. I'm fine." She spun and walked away before she was back in front of him. "I'm sorry, Buckley. That wasn't nice of me."

"It's okay, love. I understand totally." He bent to kiss her, and then sent her off to bed, knowing that he would not be sleeping. Instead, he would be spending the night on his knees by his office chair, petitioning heaven to bring his love's memory back and then protect her while they worked to find whoever it was.

Chapter 17

Charles' keen eyes watched Locklin closely the next morning as she set his mug of coffee in front of him and then a plate of oatmeal cookies that she had just made. Buckley seated her before he reached for her teapot and one of the cups and saucers, setting them down by her before his own mug of coffee was on the table and he was seated beside her.

Buckley looked between Locklin and Charles and sighed. She's out of her element, isn't she, Lord? She wasn't ready to be a minister's wife, and I forced her into that.

Charles' voice caught at his attention and he looked that way, to find Charles grinning at Locklin.

"Locklin, these are delicious. I must have the recipe. Lois has been looking for an oatmeal recipe just like these."

"Thank you, Charles. It's one I can write out for you." Her brow wrinkled. "I don't remember how I knew it. It was just there when I started."

"It's probably one that you made many times. Our hands will take over sometimes in situations like this. Buckley, do you know what a treasure you have here?" Charles nodded at Locklin's look of shock. "He does, Locklin. I can see just how well suited you two are. You are going to be a wonderful addition to our church family."

"But, I'm dangerous. I could bring someone in to harm the church."

"We know that, Locklin, and are prepared for that. As Buckley could tell you, we have sat through many meetings discussing the situations in other churches, where security was needed. We have worked with the local police and a security firm, just to be prepared. We have officers in our congregation that are there every single Sunday. Besides, God protects us, doesn't He?"

She finally nodded. "He does, but it would still be my fault."

"No, not your fault. The fault of whoever it is that is behind this. What can you tell me about what you have remembered?"

"Just bits and pieces. After our scare yesterday, I'm not sure that I want to remember."

Charles studied her. "And just what was your scare?"

"A blood-covered Teddy bear. She opened the package and screamed. Then, she remembered that she had had others of them, but today she's not remembering that she said that."

"Is that right, Locklin? How do you know that you received others?"

Locklin shook her head. "I'm not sure. I could just remember staring down at something similar to what I was holding. Only it wasn't a Teddy bear. It was a doll once. A piece of clothing, a child's sweater, I think, another time. Photos. A Bible." She looked up, surprise on her face. "How did you do that?"

"Do what?" Charles simply smiled at her.

"Get me to remember that?" She frowned at him.

Charles grinned once more. "It's only a matter of asking the questions that will help you to remember. Sometimes, it takes the questions coming from someone not close to us. Dallas would have been around, I gather. You are aware that he is a friend of the fellows here. That would make it more difficult for you to open up to him, in a way. I'm a relative stranger to you. Therefore, I can ask a question that might help you to remember."

"I see." Locklin was lost in thought at that point, not hearing Buckley and Charles talking. Her hands began to shake and then she was sinking to the floor, an exclamation from Buckley as he sprang to catch her.

"Locklin?" He called for her, not having her respond.

Charles had a cold cloth in his hand almost before Buckley had gathered her close. "Here. Use this on her face and then her wrists. We need her to come around and now." He knelt beside the younger couple, feeling for a wrist and a pulse. Charles was a retired family physician, who still kept up his skills by volunteering at the shelter.

"Locklin?" Buckley breathed a sigh of relief as her eyes opened and she stared around. "Locklin?"

His voice brought her attention to him, and she frowned. "I don't know you, do I? Where am I?" She looked around, panic in her eyes, before she looked back at him. "You're the one who stepped in and helped me. I went with you. You married me, didn't you?"

"I did, love. That I did. You remember?"

"Not a lot. I just remember running towards you but not why. I was terrified."

"You were. Do you remember the accident?"

Locklin shook her heard. "No, I don't. Is that what happened?"

"It was. Your side of the car hit the tree after the car had rolled. You lost your memory." Buckley just hugged her tight, not giving in to his fear that when she remembered everything, she would just walk away from him.

Charles stood, waiting for Buckley to stand and set Locklin on her feet. "Locklin? May I examine you? I'm a retired physician and work at the shelter. I won't hurt you. I promise. Head injuries have always been of a particular interest to me."

Locklin shrugged. "I guess. We have to go to the shelter?"

"Not at all, young lady." He simply grinned at her. "We can do it right here, or pop down to the well-stocked infirmary downstairs."

"Here, please." Her voice was barely audible and both men could see the fright in her eyes.

"Here it is." Charles finally stepped back, rubbing at his chin, his eyes on Locklin.

"Charles?" Buckley's voice finally caught his attention.

"Buckley. Locklin. What testing was done when you brought her in?"

"I can't remember. Doc would. Why?"

"Because there is something going on. Locklin, were you ever given any medications to take that you can remember?"

"I don't know. Other than the medications I was given for the headaches." Buckley was on the move, returning with it. "Thank you. This is it. I haven't been taking it much in the last three days or so."

"I see." Charles scanned the label. "I don't recognize this doctor. Who is he?"

Buckley at him. "Doc is the one who prescribed it."

Charles popped the top from the vial and looked inside. "Whatever you have been taken, it's not what is on the label. I have no idea what these tablets are." He looked at the label again. "And it's your regular pharmacy?"

"Actually, no. It's the one that was closest to here."

"I see. Buckley, this must go to Dallas. Locklin, if you have headaches, try an over-the-counter medication. If not, talk to Doc again. I'll see him today. If I have your permission, I'll talk to him."

Chapter 18

Sunday morning, Buckley turned as he heard Locklin's heels tapping on the floor as she approached him where he stood in the home office. He paused, his eyes on her face, thinking how beautiful she was, before he reached for her hands, raising them to kiss them. He stood, their hands linked, his eyes on her face, seeing her uncertainty.

"I wasn't sure what to wear, Buckley. I seem to remember just wearing jeans and a top to my old church. But I can't here." She had chosen a flowered dress that came to her mid-calf and shoes with a low heel on them.

"It wouldn't have mattered what you wore, love. We dress in all sorts of manners. Some jeans, some suits, some in-between for the men. The ladies are the same. Some wear jeans and a top, skirts, and blouses, suits. It's your choice. But you love absolutely beautiful."

She blushed. "I'm still not sure about this."

"I know, love. I know. Here's let pray first." Buckley's prayer was powerful, soothing the nerves that had wracked Locklin's body. He looked up before he dropped one hand to reach for a small box on his desk. "Here. I want you to have this. We rushed into our marriage with only the wedding bands. That didn't do justice to you." He opened the box to pull out a ruby ring. "I can remember my father telling my mother that she was his Proverbs 31 lady, that her worth was far about rubies. It is how I feel about you." The ring landed on her finger, to guard the engraved wedding band that he had chosen.

Two hours later, Locklin looked around the basement of the church, feeling somewhat overcome. She frowned as she caught sight of an older man staring at her and shivered. She spun, intent on finding Buckley, only to have her way blocked by another man. Frightened, she turned and made her way through the crowd, finding Branigan and Breck heading for her, their attention on the second man who was following her.

"Locklin? Just who we needed to see. We need to ask you something." Breck had captured her arm and led her through the crowd, towards Buckley who had been stopped by one of the other board members. "I don't think that you have met Jacob Baker."

Buckley swept her close to him, his eyes on Breck's face, and sighed. Even here, she wasn't safe. They couldn't lock the doors and keep out the strangers. And who to say one of the church members wasn't involved? That very thought frightened him.

Buckley tracked Breck down later that afternoon. Locklin was sleeping, and he felt he had to get to the bottom of what had happened in church.

"Breck? What was that about?"

Breck spun from where he stood staring out the lobby window. "Earlier? There was a man coming after Locklin. Branigan and I moved in to separate her from them. There was one after her, and one on the other side of the room, watching her. Brandon was able to snap photos of them and sent them on to Dallas and to Emma. They're trying to identify them."

Buckley paled. "In the church? With all those people? Where is she safe?"

"I don't know. I'm sorry, Buckley. It shouldn't be happening."

"It's no different for us than the others." Buckley suddenly grinned. "So, now, we know where they will try to capture her. How do we go on the offensive?"

Breck shook his head, a small smile tickling at his mouth. "Buckley, only you. You have your humour to get you through. You've done that with all of us over this. By the way, I see the garden didn't start producing fruit when you told it to."

Buckley began to laugh. "No, it didn't listen very well, did it?" He sobered. "Doc spoke with me a while ago. The medication that Locklin had been taking? One of the side effects can be memory loss. It's not a prescription drug."

"So, her prescription was tampered with? Have you talked to Dallas?"

"Not yet. I will. I thought he was away for a few days on vacation."

"That's right. He is." Breck walked back towards the stairs with Buckley. "Then, let's hope Emma can come up with something."

"She and Abe and their little one are away as well. She sent a text a while ago, stating that Jace would work on what we needed." Buckley paused, one foot on the step, his hand on the smooth oak railing. "How do I protect her? If they come into the church like that and try and take her in front of all those people, how do I do it?"

"We try and stay with you, some of us. Our ladies are invested in this as well. They want to keep her safe, knowing what they went through. They don't want that for either one of you. I spoke with Charles earlier. He has asked the officers who attend to stay by the doors for now, to monitor those coming in and out. They will be near both you and Locklin during the time you are at church." Breck held up his hand as Buckley went to protest. "I don't think you fully realize how the church feels about you. And that feeling now extends to your bride. The officers have all come forward to Charles and Barnabas stating that when you are in the church building, one will be there. If you are out and about on church business, you will have someone driving you."

Buckley swallowed hard. "Thank you. I hadn't expected this."

"It's what they want to do, Buckley. And if Locklin has to be out on her own, someone will be with her. Even on the grounds."

Locklin spoke from the step above them. "That's not fair to the men, Breck."

Breck looked up, seeing the dark shadows under her eyes. "It is fair to you and to Buckley. It's what we do, Locklin. Now, I must run. I'm off for a birthday party for a young man and I can't be late."

They watched him walk rapidly away before Locklin spoke.

"This is so unfair, Buckley. They're putting their lives at risk for us."

"I know, love. I know. But we must accept. Sometimes the givers must be receivers. I have been the one always giving. It's tough to be on the other side."

Locklin paused just inside their doorway, her face puzzled. "Buckley? Why do you call me 'love' all the time?"

"Because you are just that. My love. I haven't wanted to burden you with that. And I won't, not until you are ready. But I will still call you 'love'." He touched her cheek gently and walked away.

Staring after him, Locklin blinked back tears. "Oh, Buckley, do you know how I needed to hear that? You are my love as well. Only, I don't know how to tell you that."

Chapter 19

Hitting the outside wall of the gym hard, Buckley struggled to escape the hands holding him against it. He could feel the rough wood scraping at his face. There was no release from the hands. Then, he yelped with pain, unable to escape the board driven at the side of his knee, buckling it and dropping him to the ground. His hands clutched at it, even as another blow from the same board landed even harder on his arm. Buckley heard a snap before intense pain darkened his vision. He didn't hear the men leaving.

Sometime later, Bradon and Brennen approached the gym, joking comments tossed between the two before Brennen's hand was on Bradon's arm to stop him.

"What's that by the shrubs?" Brennen was on the run. "It's Buckley. He's been hurt."

Bradon's phone was out as he called for help, even as he dropped down beside Buckley. "They want to know if he's conscious."

"No, he's not. Let them know that." Brennen looked up. "Find someone to bring Locklin."

"Already on it. She was with the ladies today." Bradon was on his feet, running towards the building, finding Breck heading his way. "Buckley's hurt. Brennen's with him. I'm going for Locklin."

——

Breck stared after him, and then down at his phone. He had just heard from Dallas, who sent a warning that someone was after Buckley. A patrol officer had found a car near the Foundation grounds and stopped it from leaving. The men had not put up a fight, merely stating that they had been hired to scare the minister.

Locklin looked up as Bradon approached her, and then paled. She rose and went with him, listening to his explanation even as he tucked her into his truck, Ennis with them. She didn't wait for him to fully stop, shoving open the door and running into the hospital, desperately seeking Buckley. Brennen stopped her, pulling her to one side.

"Brennen?" She was frantic to hear that he was alive.

"He's been hurt, Locklin. He was ambushed near the gym. I'm not sure yet what his injuries are, but we'll find out. Doc's on duty today. Here, sit." Brennen made Locklin sit, even though he could tell that she was about to refuse to do that.

"How?" Her voice died away and then she tried again. "How bad?"

"The paramedics said his arm and his leg. We'll know more in a bit." He looked up as Jaxcy sat beside Locklin, an arm around her. "We're not leaving you alone, Locklin. One of us goes with you when you go back. Dallas is on his way here. Apparently, he was to meet with you today. He had just talked to Buckley as he was walking to the gym."

"And then this happened. When does it stop, Jaxcy? Ennis? When does it stop? When one of us is dead? Oh! I wish I could remember!" Her voice died away as she paled. "It's him. There. By the door. He's the one who was chasing me. Make him go away."

Brennen shifted in his chair, searching for the man, his eye catching Dallas, who nodded and moved towards the man, preventing him from leaving. A short struggle ensued and then Dallas had the man handcuffed and handed over to a patrol officer.

Locklin had paled even more. The ones with her could her low whisper and looked at one another.

Dallas crouched down in front of her. "Locklin? What was it that you just said?"

"He told Buckley that I was his. That I had to go with him. He tried to hit Buckley but Buckley moved and the man ended up on the ground. I don't know why he said that. I have such fear when I see him. And I don't know why." Locklin looked up. "I am starting to remember things, Dallas, but not enough to put together anything."

"It's coming, Locklin. Maybe if you took a notebook and wrote down the bits and pieces, we can put them together for you."

"I can try, but a lot of times it's in my dreams. And then I can't remember if it was a dream or real life."

"I don't think that matters right now, Locklin." Ennis' arm was around her. "Just write down everything. We'll sort it out for you."

Locklin finally rose to pace, unable to stay in one position for long. Brennen paced on one side of her, Blair on the other, no one wanting her to be on her own and vulnerable. She had looked up at them with a slight smile. Blair had drawn in a quick breath at the whiteness of her face and the dark smudges under her eyes.

Ennis studied her as well. "She's not sleeping."

"No, I don't think she is. She said Doc wanted to give her something but she refused." Fynn looked around. "I think everyone is here."

"They would be. They would do no less for Buckley and his Locklin." Cadee watched the men milling around. "They're working on it. Why don't we work on it as well? We would have a different perspective than them."

"You mean, from a female point of view?" Guenivere nodded. "I agree. I talked to Emma's friend, Kataleen. She asked if we had any more information on Locklin, other than what we had given Emma."

"I don't think that we have. This has to be so frustrating for them." Berneen rose, heading for the gift shop, and returned with note pads and pens. "Here. One for each of us. Now, let's start sleuthing."

Locklin had dropped back in her chair, taking what was handed to her, a frown on her face. "And just how do we do that?"

"You start by jotting down everything you remember, no matter how minor it seems. It is sometimes something so minor that breaks a case."

Hagen studied her and then frowned as she saw Charles and his wife entering. She drew in her breath as she stared between Locklin and Lois. She was on her feet, heading for Brandon. "Brandon, did we ever figure out if Locklin had any aunts or uncles?"

"I'm not the one working on it. Brody was. Brody? Did you ever determine if there are relatives for Locklin?"

"I did. Her mother had a sister who lives around here. Why?" Brody stood beside them, a puzzled look on his face.

Hagen turned towards Lois. "Take a look at Lois and then Locklin. What do you see?"

The men frowned at her before they did just that. Brody drew in a breath before he shared a look with Brandon.

"Emma. She could tell us." Brody's phone was out, sending off a quick message to Emma, who responded quickly. "Emma has tracked down the sister. She lives here." Brody froze, unable to continue.

"Brody? Is it that bad?" Hagen couldn't understand his stillness.

"She's Lois."

"Lois?" Brandon spun around once more to stare at Lois and Charles. "As is Charles' wife?"

"Exactly. Now how do we do this?" Brody watched as Locklin rose, heading for the exam rooms as Doc approached her, Dallas and Breck on either side of her.

Chapter 20

Locklin stared down at Buckley, watching his beloved face contorting with pain as he moved before he laid still. Her hand was against his cheek in an effort to still his movements.

"Doc?" She looked up at him. "What is wrong with him?"

"A broken arm. And a heavy bruise on his knee. That will take time to heal."

"So, what happens now?"

"Right now, the orthopedic surgeon will set his arm. He can do that without Buckley heading for surgery. The knee will be in a brace for a few days. He can't weight bear for about a week." Doc watched as Locklin's eyes slid closed and a single tear tracked down her cheek. "He'll use a wheelchair for that and then he can start weight bearing using a cane."

Locklin nodded, watching the activity around Buckley. "I want to stay with him. Please?"

"For now. But when they go to set the arm, you'll have to leave." Doc nodded at Breck as he walked away.

Dallas stood beside Brody, shock on his face. "Who did you say?"

"Lois. Take a look at her."

Dallas turned. "You're right. She does look like her. Where's the proof?"

"Check your emails. Emma was sending it on to you." Brody watched as Dallas did just that. "Now, we need to talk to both of them."

"We do. Right now, Locklin's not up to it. I want to talk to both Buckley and her together."

The men looked up as Charles and Lois approached.

"Brody, keep us updated, please? We'll be praying for both of them."

Lois nodded before she spoke. "This young lady? She looks familiar. Do I know her?"

"Locklin? I don't think so." Brody was careful about how he phrased his words.

"Locklin?" Lois paled. "My sister's baby was named Locklin. It's such an unusual name. Where is she?"

"Right here." Locklin stood beside Brody, finding his arm around her and Hagen on her other side. "Why?"

Lois paled even more. "You are the image of my sister. Your mother? Is she still alive?"

"No, I'm told that she isn't. Again, why?"

"Because you are the image of my sister. Oh, please, dear Lord. Let this be our Locklin, our Laycee's girl."

"Laycee?" Locklin began to shake before she whispered. "I remember. Laycee was my mother's name. Are you her sister?"

"I am. Oh, thank you, dear Lord." Lois simply swept Locklin into a tight hug, tears flowing down her cheeks.

Charles stood watching before he turned to Dallas. "How sure are we?"

"Fairly sure. I was hoping to talk with Buckley and Locklin together before we approached you. It looks as if the Lord had other plans."

"He did. Lois has prayed for years to find Locklin. She lost contact with Locklin's father just after her sister died. She would write, try to call, but received no answer. We even went to their home area a few times but couldn't track them down."

"You did? That's interesting. Charles, we will need to talk with you then. I'll call and set up a time." Dallas had pulled out his phone as it chimed. "I'm sorry. I need to run. Brody, have someone keep me updated on Buckley."

Locklin abruptly moved away from Lois, heading back towards where Buckley was. She just needed to talk to him, and not likely could. Standing in the hallway, she watched through the open door as the surgeon set his arm, the staff moving around her. She never noticed Breck and Blair standing beside her, their attention on the people around them.

The surgeon studied her as he left Buckley's bedside and then beckoned her forward.

———

"You're Buckley's wife. I thought I recognized you from Sunday. Here, in you go. He's been awake for a bit. I've ordered some pain medications for him. He can go home tonight. I know the building and that Doc and Brady will be around to make sure that you don't need anything."

"Doctor? How bad?" Locklin could barely get the words out.

"The arm? It will take about six weeks or so to heal. It was a clean break. The knee? I want to do an MRI on it next week. We need to let some of the swellings go down first. The nurse will make sure that you have everything that you need." He paused, his eyes on her pale face. "Locklin, he will heal."

"I know, but it's my fault. I did this to him." Her words were barely audible as she moved away from the men and towards Buckley.

"What did she say?" The surgeon stared after her.

"She's convinced that it's her fault. She can't remember a lot right now, but Buckley stepped in to help her when she was in danger."

"Just like all of you fellows from the building. Make sure that he follows my instructions. I know him. He'll be chafing at the bit to get back to work."

"That we will. We will do our best." Breck stepped into the room, Blair on his heels. "We need to set up for him in the apartment. Thank goodness the doors are built for handicap accessibility."

"There's that. I'm off then, Breck. Call if you need something."

"We will. Thanks, Blair. Send the others home, will you?"

"I can do that. Brennen said he was staying to help with moving Buckley home."

"Thank him for me. I have no idea when that will be."

Chapter 21

Frowning in frustration, Buckley pushed at the wheel of the chair he was in, not happy that he couldn't move himself forward. Locklin had stood back, not ready to move, but finally did just that, pushing him into the living room and positioning the chair so that he could slide to the couch. This takes a lot of effort, Buckley thought, and laid his head back for a moment, feeling a blanket tucked over him before he heard Locklin moving away.

Locklin returned, a tray in her hands that she set on the coffee table, before she dropped to the floor, an arm resting on the couch seat beside him.

"What can I get for you, Buckley?"

"I'm not sure, Locklin. You're okay? They didn't get to you?" Buckley had been worried when he had awakened at last late the afternoon before in the hospital, looking around for her.

"No, the fellows and Dallas kept me safe." She bit at her lip, a habit that Buckley noticed she had when she was uncertain.

"What happened, love?" He reached for her hand. "Tell me."

"The man that you saved me from? I recognized him. He was in the waiting room, watching me. Dallas arrested him."

"He was? That's not good. I'm glad he didn't get to you." Buckley waited for her to continue. "What else happened, love? Something did."

Locklin nodded. "I was so worried when they came to get me. I couldn't get you to talk to me at all. And then I remembered my mother's name. Did you know that Lois, Charles' wife, was her sister?"

Buckley started and then nodded. "I wondered who she reminded me of. It is you. You've met her?"

"They were there. She asked who my mother was." Locklin blinked back tears. "That Emma had confirmed it already. Lois said that they tried to find me or Dad, and couldn't."

"So, whatever this is goes back that far?" Buckley whistled. "Wow! Who would have thought that?"

"I don't like it, Buckley. I mean, she says that she's my aunt, and we do look somewhat alike, but I just can't do this. Not right now. You need me. I can't remember a lot."

"I know, love. Charles and Lois will stay back, now that they've made contact. I suspect that Lois will send you photos and a long letter. It's how she is, but they will wait for you to approach them."

"They will? That's strange."

"It's how they are. What else happened?"

Locklin handed him his mug of coffee, trying to think about how to frame what she needed to say.

"The ladies told me to journal what I remember, whether I think it's a dream or not."

"That's a good idea. Have you a journal?"

"I do. Berneen bought one for each of us and a pen as well. She shouldn't have."

"That's Berneen. She gives and gives, without expecting anything in return. I think you should. If you want, we can go over it together."

Locklin's head went down against his good leg, her eyes on him, the trust she felt in him showing as well as the growing love she had for him. "I would like that. Buckley, where do we go from here?"

"With the investigation?" At her nod, he shook his head. "I'm not sure. Dallas is working on it. Emma and Jace are. So are the fellows. And I suspect that the ladies are, if Berneen had bought you all notebooks."

"That's what they want to do. I just don't want anyone hurt. Not one person. It's bad enough that we have been."

"I know, love. It's hard, but they won't think anything of it. We've all been there for each other."

"I get that." Locklin grew quiet and her face pensive as she studied Buckley. "Buckley, what is God trying to teach us?"

"Teach us? As in what can we learn by going through this?"

Locklin nodded. "I have this vision of a conversation with my father. I think that I had been questioning something. Dad told me that God was there with us all the time. That sometimes He allowed things or events to happen, just to draw us closer to Him. To teach us that we need to trust and rely on Him and not ourselves."

"Your father sounds like a very wise man. That's what I believe."

"Is it? Is that how we look at things? It's hard."

"It is very hard when we try to do it in our humanness. We need to set that aside and realize that it is in God's strength that we do that."

She nodded, her eyes closing as she slept. Buckley pulled himself up as best he could to reach for the blanket to drape over her before he laid back himself, his eyes closing as he prayed for his love.

Locklin rose an hour later, her eyes on Buckley as he slept, the blanket that he had used to cover her now over him. Tray in her hands, she headed for the kitchen, as a knock came on the door. She stood on tiptoes to peer out, before opening it, to find Breck, Blair, and Devaney there.

"Come in. Buckley's sleeping." Locklin waited for one of them to speak. "What? No one talking? If you're not talking, I'm going to go clean my kitchen."

Devaney gave a low laugh, linking her arm with Locklin's. "And I will help. These two guys can see to Buckley."

Locklin looked back at them before she shook her head. "If they want. I still have to make us lunch."

Chapter 22

A week later, Buckley sighed as he sat at his desk in the church office. Locklin had driven him there, against the protests of some of the fellows. She had simply stared them down, slipped behind the wheel of his car, and driven away.

"Did you really just do that?" Buckley grinned at her.

"Do what?" Locklin was distracted, staring at all the books he had on the shelves.

"Drive away from them? They were supposed to come with us."

She shrugged. "You needed to be here. It would have taken forever for them to decide who was coming with us."

"I know, love, but we really should have waited." Buckley turned his attention to his desk, sorting through the mail. He was lost in his work in short order, a quiet thank you as Locklin set a mug of coffee beside him. He finally looked up, finding her curled up in a chair, a book open on her knee that she wasn't reading.

"Locklin?" He had to say her name twice before she looked over at him. "You're deep in thought."

"I know. I'm thinking about Lois. She says that she's my aunt. Emma sent me documents that prove it.

But I just don't see it. How could she lose contact with my Dad?"

"That's what the fellows are working on. You have doubts?"

"I do. I know that they're part of the church family, and I don't want to cause any trouble in it, but I just don't know."

"What is it that is troubling you?" Buckley was willing to take the time to draw her out.

"I'm not sure. I think I need to talk to someone, but I'm not sure who. Someone who would understand about families and family relationships and family trees."

Buckley reached for his phone. "I know just the person. One of Abe's men and his wife. She is into family trees and has a wonderful program that she developed." He paused, looking up at Locklin in surprise. "I have an email from Micah. His wife is Kataleen, who I just described. They are on their way here, this afternoon." Buckley looked down at his work.

Locklin was on her feet, her hands reaching to help him. "Tell me what I can do for you that's not breaching any confidences. There must be something."

"There is." Buckley quickly sorted through what he had on his desk and together they worked away.

"It looks as if we've made good progress." Locklin stood, a hand on his shoulder.

"We have, love. It's at a point where I can leave it for tonight and come back tomorrow to work more." Buckley stood, sweeping her into a hug and then kissing her. "Thank you, love."

Locklin blushed, not sure still if he really meant it when he called her love. "Now, let's get you home. This friend of yours? They're going to the building?"

"I would expect so. Here, let me lock up the office."

They walked out slowly, Buckley giving more of an overview of the congregation to her, just to help her understand.

Micah watched as Buckley made his way towards him as he stood in the building lobby, Kataleen beside him.

"That's Locklin?" Kataleen studied her. "She's just what he needs."

"That she is, sweetheart. The men have all said that." Micah reached to shake Buckley's hand, waiting for the introduction to Locklin.

Kataleen reached to hug Locklin. "I've been waiting to meet you. We all wondered who Buckley's lady would be. You're perfect for him." She grinned as Locklin finally remembered to shut her mouth. "Now, where can we go to talk?"

"Our apartment, unless you want to head for the conference room?" Buckley shared a look with Micah.

"Your apartment is good." Micah grinned as he held up a plastic sack. "We stopped and bought some submarine sandwiches, some salads, and some fresh fruit. How does that sound for a meal?"

"It sounds wonderful. Slavedriver here didn't let me have a break all afternoon." Locklin smirked as she headed into the kitchen, reaching to start the coffee and then put on the kettle. Kataleen searched for plates and cutlery, laughing at Locklin's nonsense and at Buckley's laughing protest that she hadn't told him that she wanted a break.

Buckley finally pushed his plate away, reaching for Locklin's hand. "Let's spend some time in prayer. I have a feeling we'll need it."

"I think that you're correct. Kataleen has found a lot of information, some of which she has confirmed."

"But I'm not sure if I can help. I still can't remember a lot."

"That's okay, Locklin. We'll work with what we can."

Chapter 23

Buckley fingered the papers that Micah had left with him, not able to sleep. As she had stated, Locklin had not been able to confirm much of what Kataleen had found. It had frustrated her, that much he knew. He sat at his office desk, reading back through every piece of paper, tracing the family tree that Kataleen had drawn up. He shook his head, not knowing how she could do that. It had to be God, he thought.

Locklin rose early in the morning, frowning as she saw the light on in the office. Searching for Buckley, she found him deep into his study on prayer, the papers set aside. Her hand on his shoulder roused him and he swept her down on his knee, despite her protest that he would be hurt.

"You didn't sleep?"

"No, I didn't. I was going over what Kataleen left and then turned to read on prayer. I'm thinking that it would make a good series."

"It would. I feel like such a baby when it comes to prayer. I pray for this to be over, but it's not."

"I know, love. I do the same. God is working on this, but sometimes His timing is not our timing."

"I wish He would hurry up and get it over." Locklin sounded disgruntled. "I'm sorry. I shouldn't have said that."

"And why not? He listens to us and wants to hear our joys and our hurts. This is one of your hurts."

"And yours?" Locklin poked at the papers. "Did you find anything in there?"

"I did. I was waiting to talk to you. We need to turn it over to the fellows as well."

"And?"

"I found your mother didn't have a sister. She had a cousin, who was raised as a sister to her. That was Lois. I'm not sure why Lois wouldn't have known that." Buckley frowned. "We need to talk to them."

"Let's do some more research before you do. I don't want to hurt her. Kataleen mentioned that last night. You and Micah had stepped outside when she did. I thought that you would have heard."

"No, I didn't. That's okay. We'll get there. Anything else that stands out?"

"My father. He had siblings and they must have had children. How do I confirm that? Kataleen said that she couldn't give me that information, as it wasn't ethical."

"I see. Then, we turn this over to Dallas and see what he can find out for you."

"Poor Dallas. He's had so much thrown at him. He told me that he's working a lot of cases now."

"I know. I feel bad that he's involved in this." Buckley finally stood, his hand reaching for hers. "Let's eat and then head downstairs."

Brendon looked at Buckley and then at the paperwork that Buckley was handing him.

"Kataleen? They were around yesterday?"

"They were. They were here long enough to eat and go over this with us."

"I see. Anything we need to watch for?"

Buckley explained what he had discovered and what they were trying to discover. "Locklin still hasn't remembered that much."

"That worries me, Buckley. It's like she's blocking it."

"I know. I had a long discussion with Doc. He said it's likely that she is blocking some of it, knowing it will hurt her deeply. I don't want that, but I want her to remember."

"I know, Buckley. She's off with the ladies?"

"She is. Berneen handed them all notebooks and a pen. They're racing us to try and solve this."

Brendon grinned. "And it wouldn't surprise me if they did just that. I'll make copies. You get off your feet. Do you have to head to the church office?"

"Not right at the moment. I'm working from home for today." Buckley walked away, his limp very evident that day.

"He's hurting." Blair stood and watched him.

"He is. He's not joking with us like he usually does." Brendon looked down at the paperwork in his hand. "Kataleen did some of her magic and dropped it off last night. I guess this just adds to our work."

Brady reached for it. "Let me make copies. Burnie should be here. This is what he enjoys."

"He's back tomorrow. He had no choice. His publisher wanted him to do that book signing." Benen headed for his favourite chair.

"I know. He hates that." Brandon sat. "Let's see how far we can get. I'm told that the ladies will solve it before us. I think that they just challenged us."

Chapter 24

Staring down at the envelope in her hand, Locklin shuddered. She knew the handwriting. It was his. How had he found her married name? And her address? She spun and ran for the conference room, seeking Buckley.

The men who were there spun as the door flew open and then were on their feet, moving towards her.

"Locklin?" Blair reached for her arm to steady her.

"Buckley? Where is he?"

"He's in the apartment. He's working there." Blair reached for the envelope in her hand. "What's this?"

"It was in the mail." Locklin's words tripped over each other, she was that frantic and terrified. "It's him. He has found me."

"Who, Locklin? Who has found you?"

"I don't know his name. He kept watching me. He'd follow me all over. Please? Make him stop! Please? Don't let him near me!" Her eyes rolled back as she collapsed, Brady reaching for her before he headed for the stairs and the apartment, Locklin in his arms.

Buckley stared at Brady and then at Locklin. "What happened?"

"She fainted, Buckley. She received a letter, came looking for you, and then collapsed. She recognized the handwriting."

"She did?" Buckley sat on the couch, Locklin's head on his knee, even as Brady crouched down beside her to assess her.

"She did. She was terrified, Buckley. Kept asking us to stop him and to keep him away from her."

"She did? Had she opened it?"

"No, she just was holding it away from her. It needs to go to Dallas. Blair was calling him but he couldn't reach him."

Blair extended the letter. "This is it, Buckley. I'd leave it for Dallas."

"I intend to." Buckley nodded at the table. "Drop it there. Thanks, fellows."

"No problem. Let us know what Dallas says."

"I will." Buckley heard the door close behind them, but his attention was on Locklin. His heart broke for his lady, wanting to make it all better for her, but not able to. Lord? How long? How long until this is over for her? How much more hurt and danger will she face? Teach us, Lord, to pray, to pray as we should, that Your will be done. Protect us, dear Lord.

Locklin roused in the late afternoon, disoriented. She rose, wandering the apartment, frightened. She couldn't find someone to help her. Why not? She wasn't in her own apartment. Where was she? Hearing a sound behind her, Locklin spun, a hand covering her mouth to stifle her scream.

"Locklin, love? You're up?" Buckley moved towards her, stopping as she backed away from him. "Locklin?"

"I'm sorry. I'm sorry. I shouldn't have run to you that day. Forgive me?" She turned and ran, for where she wasn't sure, Buckley moving after her as quickly as he could, his arms reaching to sweep her to him.

She fought him until she heard his whispered prayer and then his words of love whispered in her ear. Locklin looked up, her heart calming.

"Buckley?"

"Locklin? You worried me. Are you okay?" Buckley's head tilted as he studied her

"I think so. I just didn't know where I was. I wasn't in my own apartment. I forgot for a bit. Forgive me?"

"There's nothing to forgive. Here, let's sit. You're shaking." Buckley directed her back to the couch, wrapping her in a blanket and just sitting close to her, holding her tight.

"I'm sorry, Buckley. I'm sorry I brought danger to you. I shouldn't have."

"I could have walked away, Locklin, but it's not in me to do that to anyone, let alone a lady I love."

Locklin stared up at him, her eyes wide. "You love me?"

"I do, Locklin. You are the other half of my heart. God sent me there that day. I had no plans to head that way. I was on vacation and just took off."

"Then, God was in control." She leaned against him. "He really does care."

"And you didn't think that He did?"

Her head shook. "No, I didn't. I mean, I knew in my head that He does. Sometimes, the heart has trouble understanding that."

"It does, but never doubt that God loves you and wants to protect you. He may let us go through rough stuff, like we are now, but unless He wills otherwise, we won't die."

"That's a comfort." Locklin looked around. "The letter?"

"Dallas was here while you were sleeping. He said not to awaken you. He didn't open it, not yet. He was turning it over to the techs and letting them do that. He'll call us with what they found, but it might be tomorrow."

"I felt such evil when I was holding it. I couldn't pray, I really couldn't even think."

"The fellows said you were upset. I can see why." Buckley grew silent, content to sit and hold her.

"Buckley, that family tree? It's accurate?"

"It is. Kataleen is very careful not to include something or someone that she can't confirm. If it's there, then she had made sure it is accurate. You're questioning something?"

"No. I've just never seen a family tree before. Not for my own family. And Lois? Have you talked to her?"

"Not yet. I was waiting for Emma and Kataleen to provide more information, just as they promised. Then, I'll meet with Charles and Lois. Talk to them. See where we go. You're not going to be there, not now. Not until you can remember much more than you have."

"Thank you. I just don't think I can handle that right now. When she hugged me and cried, I didn't feel anything. Is that wrong of me?"

"She is a stranger to you. It's normal not to feel a lot in that situation."

"Okay. I just don't want to hurt her. If she really is Mom's sister or cousin, she's been hurt enough."

"I know, love. I know. We'll get through it. Blair was around as well. He has more information that he wants to go over with us, but I said not until tomorrow. And then tomorrow night, we have our prayer meeting at the church."

"We do? I think I need that." She was quiet.

"You can wear jeans, love. You don't have to be dressed up. In fact, most of the time that's what I'm in. Our church doesn't stress that you have to dress a certain way. The person is more important than the clothes that they wear. They feel it is more in line with how Jesus would approach people, given that he could be found with the outcasts of society in the Bible."

"That's so true and so comforting." She settled back, her head on his shoulder, content to be held.

Chapter 25

Two weeks later, Buckley watched as the cast was removed from his arm, Locklin tight to his side, her own eyes on the surgeon. He had healed extremely fast, the surgeon had declared. Buckley had grinned, shaken his head, and said that he always healed quickly.

Hand in hand, they walked away from the hospital, towards Buckley's car, not seeing the man following them. Would it have changed anything, if they had, Buckley wondered afterward? He was never sure. Dallas had asked to meet with them that morning, as he had news.

Dallas seated them at a table in a small conference room in the police department and then sat himself, a thick file folder in front of him. Buckley sent a questioning look his way but Dallas' attention was on Locklin.

"Locklin? Have you remembered anything else?"

Locklin stared at him, a frown on her face. "Not really. Just bits and pieces and even those don't make a lot of sense. I can't tell if it's real or a dream."

Dallas nodded. "That's what we thought." He tapped the folder. "Your friend, Emma, has been sending massive amounts of information, Buckley. I don't know how she does it, but she does. Will has

122

finally managed to have her come on as a consultant with us."

"And that helps?"

"It does. She has provided more information about your father, Locklin, that we can't divulge to you as yet as it is still part of an ongoing investigation."

Locklin frowned. "I don't remember Dad. When did he die again?"

"About a year or less ago. He was murdered. Do you remember us talking about that?"

She nodded. "I do. And you said Mom died in childbirth. I have no siblings. What else?"

"You are twenty-eight years old. You worked odd jobs to survive. Your church was an important part of your life, but you didn't involve yourself in a lot of activities outside of the normal services. I have had conversations with your pastor there. The fire that destroyed your apartment building was deemed accidental. Plumbers were there, to do work on some of the pipes." He paused as she shook her head.

"No, I can remember the landlord. A slumlord, is that what you call them? I can remember that he refused to do any work for us, even when the furnace failed in the middle of winter. We had to go to a lawyer and threaten him with a lawsuit. Even then, it took a while for him to have it repaired."

"Is that right?" Dallas looked down at his notes. "Someone didn't explain that very well to us, then. We talked to the other tenants. They could not say enough good about him."

"He would threaten us." Locklin looked at Buckley, a bleak look on her face. "He would threaten us. I can remember that. We would come home and our doors would be unlocked, our belongings thrown all over the place. There were would be things missing. We found threats written in paint on our walls that we had to paint over. Furniture would be damaged." She dropped her head, her hair hiding her face. "I tried to move, to find somewhere else to live. I couldn't. If he found out, he would go to the new landlord and I wouldn't get the place. I had no transportation to leave town. They had taken Dad's car, saying it wasn't safe to be driven. But it was. Dad kept it up." Locklin didn't realize how much she was remembering.

Buckley's hand grasped hers tightly. "Okay, so the landlord burned the place down, or had it burned down? He can be charged?"

"We'll certainly work that way. Locklin, you have remembered things. Do you realize that?" Dallas watched her reaction closely.

Locklin shook her head. "It's as I said. It's bits and pieces. It's like I'm talking and saying things but I don't remember them if I stop and think about it. Does that make sense?"

"It does. Now, that letter that you received?" As she looked at him, he shared a look with Buckley. "You recognized the handwriting?"

"I'm told I did. I was just so scared. I don't remember even what I said that day." She looked at Buckley. "Brady told me that I fainted, and I don't faint. That's the fear I can remember. It just took over my whole body."

"She was shuddering, Dallas, in a way that I have never seen before. I want this over."

"I know you do. You fellows always do. We still have work to do. And I know you are working on it." He glanced down at the letter, reluctant to tell Locklin what it said, but knowing that he had to.

"What does it say, Dallas?" Buckley kept his eyes on Locklin.

"I won't go into all the details, but it is a direct threat to her life. It states that they know where she is and that when she least expects it, they will take her and kill her. We have an idea who it came from, and they're part of a vicious group of men. Multiple detachments are working together to bring them down. I can't begin to tell you that you must stay safe, Locklin. Stay around the building as much as you can. Stay with someone. We're working hard to bring these men down, have been for months now. It should be soon, but you're now part of it, because of your father."

"I see." Locklin shoved back from the table and stood, feeling vulnerable and overwhelmed. "Can I leave, Dallas?" Her voice was barely above a whisper.

Dallas stood. "You can, Locklin. Buckley, you too must be very cautious. They have proven that they will go after you to get to her."

"That's what they always do. Go after the one to get to the other. God is in control, Dallas. I have His protection, no matter what happens."

Chapter 26

Her hand tight in Buckley's, Locklin walked the downtown area, stopping every once in a while to study the merchandise in the windows. Buckley was content to let her, but his focus was also on those around him. He could feel someone watching them and that frightened him. He knew that they shouldn't be doing their walk, but they both needed some normalcy in their lives.

Locklin paused in front of a bakeshop, her hand resting lightly on the window, as she studied the wares.

"We can get some if you like." Buckley's voice above her startled her.

"No, it's okay. I think that I like to bake. I was just curious to see what they offered."

"Now, you know. I have a fairly well-stocked cupboard for baking. I like doing that." He grinned at her. "But for now, how be we head home?"

"We can. You need to finish preparing for your prayer meeting, don't you?"

"Not really. I mean, I'm there and lead it, but we usually just share what's on our hearts. Sometimes, I give a short talk on a subject or a verse. Other times we don't. It's working out well doing that. We are growing closer together."

"I see. I didn't realize that you didn't bring a sermon or whatever it is you call those." She frowned as he laughed.

"It's called a sermon or a message." He slid into the car, having shut her door behind her. "Some people refer to them as talks. I like to think of them as God's speaking to us. I'm just the instrument that He uses. And I'm not the only one."

"No, he uses so many. The ladies have been talking, you know." Locklin smirked as she stared out the side window. "I hear that you suggested dates for a couple of them to marry."

Buckley shouted with laughter, bringing a smile to her face. "They did, did they? I did, and they came right back at me with my own words."

"Serves you right." Locklin sobered. "Buckley, what if we never find out who it is?"

"We will, love. I am confident in that. Dallas seems to think that it would not be long." Buckley parked in his allotted spot on the Foundation grounds and shifted to watch her.

"I know, Buckley. I'm just so scared that someone will get hurt because of me. Or disappear and not be seen." She looked up at him, her eyes dark with her emotions. "I worry about Hagen's little ones."

"They'll watch them closely." He reached for her hands, his head bowing as he prayed for her and for himself.

Late that night, Locklin shot up in bed, drenched in sweat, her hands covering her mouth as she stifled a scream. He was here, wasn't he? He was here in her apartment. She knew he was. He had done that before to her. She would awaken to find him standing in her doorway, or see him disappearing out of the door.

She was out of her bed, running to check the locks on the doors and the windows, spinning in a wild circle as she searched for him, not finding him. But she knew that he had been there. She felt him.

Buckley watched for a moment from his office doorway before he carefully approached Locklin, not sure what had happened. Locklin turned to him as she heard his footsteps, backing away until she recognized his voice and form and then throwing herself at him.

"He was here, Buckley. Here in the apartment." Her sobs shook him.

"Hush, Locklin. It's just us here. No one else." He lifted her into his arms and carried her back into the office, dropping to the couch he had there and wrapping her into a blanket. His own tears wet her hair as his fear for her grew. Her sobs gradually lessened and her body grew heavy as she slept. Buckley watched her, his arms tight around her, his heart praying.

Early the next morning, Locklin slipped from his arms and headed for a shower and to dress, stopping on her way by to the kitchen to watch him, reaching to cover him with the blanket he had used for her. A quick kiss was dropped on his cheek, and she touched the roughness of the overnight growth of whiskers with a gentle hand.

Buckley shot up, suddenly awake, sure that he had heard Locklin call for him. He was on his feet, searching, finding her in the kitchen, engrossed in baking. He smiled as he watched her before she looked up.

"I'm sorry! I keep saying that." Locklin was frustrated. She had had enough of her life as she had been living it the last while. She had made some determinations that she needed to talk to Buckley about, but she was too shy with him to do just that.

"Don't be." Buckley grinned at her. "Just tell what you're making?"

"A mess, I think." Locklin looked down at the countertop. "I wanted to make some pancakes but I can't remember the recipe. I couldn't find a cookbook."

"That's because I don't have any." Buckley simply wrapped her into his arms. "I have prepared pancake mix if that will do."

"There's such a thing? I thought you could only make them from scratch." Locklin stood, shutting down.

"Locklin? Love, please talk to me." Buckley shook her slightly, finding her coming back around. "What just happened?"

"I don't know, Buckley. I don't know. All of a sudden, I just couldn't hear or understand. Some days, I feel like I am on a precipice ready to jump off."

"I know, love. I know. Here, you sit. I'll make us something." Buckley swiftly cleaned the counter, keeping an eye on her, before he simply made them toast and set it in front of her.

"I can't, Buckley. I need to be doing something or have to be somewhere. Only, I don't know where that is. Please, help me!"

"I will, love. Here, have some toast." Buckley felt out of his depth right then, watching Locklin. This is too much for her, Lord. I think I am losing her.

Chapter 27

Slowly closing the door to the church, Buckley turned to walk down the stairs, his keys in his hand, lost in thought. It had troubled him that morning by what Locklin had said. I don't know how to reach her, Lord. How do I? I pray and pray but can't reach her. She's blocking something and I don't know what.

His mind on Locklin, he didn't hear the running footsteps approaching him until he was on the ground, his keys flying from his hand. Stunned, he didn't hear the questions thundering at him, just felt himself yanked to his feet and propelled forward. His vision blurry, he didn't realize that he was being forced into the back of a truck until he hit the seat. He turned, trying to fight his way back out, but his movements still as he saw the knife held up towards him, the sunlight winking of the long, silver, sharpened blade. Buckley sank back, his hands in the air, waiting for the knife to come towards him. He kept his eyes on it even as the truck moved away from the church, his car following.

Locklin paced the apartment living room, her arms wrapped around herself, watching the clock. Buckley had promised to be home an hour ago, and he still wasn't. She began to fear for him, and ran for her phone, dialling his number and only getting his voice mail. She tried the church number and again, only got through to the voice mail.

Running for the stairs, Locklin headed downstairs, intent of searching the parking lot. He had to be here somewhere, she thought. But where? She shoved the door open, her hand up to shelter her eyes as she searched. Not finding him, she moved in a circle, fear coursing through her. They had to have taken him. But just who were they? Did she know who they were?

She walked slowly back towards the building, not seeing the car approaching her, a sound at the last minute raising her head as she screamed. The car moved slightly towards her, the fender driving into her body and sending her flying through the air, to lay, a crumpled broken heap on the pavement as it turned and sped away, almost colliding with Breck's truck as he approached.

Breck slammed on his brakes, his arm along the back of his seat, as he stared after the car. Shaking his head, he turned back to drive forward, once more slamming on his brakes and then slamming the truck into park and throwing open his door. He ran towards Locklin even as Brody and Baird ran from the building.

"What happened?" Breck's words were sharp.

"We have no idea. We heard Locklin scream and ran for the door, just in time to see the car take off. Did it hit you?"

"No, but it came close." Breck was on his knees. "Did someone call it in?"

"Berneen was." Baird was down on the ground as well. "Locklin? Can you hear us?"

"She's not responding." Breck ran his hands over her arms and legs. "I don't feel anything broken here."

"She bleeding from her head." Baird bent over until his own head almost touched the ground. "Oh, no, Dear Lord. Please!"

"Baird?" When he didn't answer, Brody's hand hit his back. "What you do see?"

"Blood. From her ear." Baird straightened back up. "You know what that means."

"We do." Breck stood up and moved back as the paramedics ran towards them. "She was run down about ten to fifteen minutes ago. We didn't see it. Baird here says that she's bleeding from her ear."

The paramedics nodded, working quickly to assess her, reaching for the neck collar and the backboard, shifting her gently to that, before one of them reached to start an IV drip. The three men helped to lift her to the stretcher and then stood back. Breck moved forward suddenly.

"Wait! I'm riding with you! She needs one of us with her."

"Is she married?"

"She is. Buckley Cullen."

"Buckley? Where is he?" The paramedic ducked to look out the window on the back door.

"That's what we don't know. He wasn't around." Breck's phone was out as he called Buckley. "No answer." He sent a swift text to Baird and then to

Barnabas. "I'll have Barnabas meet us at the hospital. He's power of attorney after Buckley."

Barnabas hit the Emergency Room doors on the run, heading for the exam rooms, finding Breck moving towards him on swift feet.

"Breck? What happened?"

"As far as we can tell, Locklin was run down in our parking lot. They almost nailed me on the way out. I wish I had known. I would have gone after them." Breck hit the wall with his fist, anger at the men flaring.

"You didn't know. Were you able to get any description?"

"Not much of one. They were moving too fast. I passed it on to the patrol officer." Breck pointed behind him. "She's in rough shape, Barnabas."

"I see. Have they said anything yet?"

"No. They wanted to talk to Buckley. We can't find him."

"What?" Barnabas paused in his pacing. "He was at the church earlier. I saw his car as I drove by."

"It's not there now. He's not anywhere around. And he's not answering his phone or text messages."

"The fellows are searching?"

"They are, as best they can. So are the patrol officers. Dallas was in touch. He's tied up on a case and can't make it here yet." Breck looked behind him as he heard the door swish open. "There's the nurse. She was looking for you about ten minutes ago."

"Heidi?" Barnabas walked towards her, a hand on Breck's arm pulling him along.

"Barnabas? I understand that you have power of attorney for Locklin Cullen?"

"I do. We're not certain where her husband is at the moment. Do you need me to sign or authorize something?"

"We do. Dr. James will be along in just a moment." Heidi stopped at a door. "In there. I must warn you, she's in rough shape, Barnabas."

Breck caught the look that Heidi had on her face that Barnabas didn't see and his heart sank. They don't expect her to make it, do they, Lord? Please, Lord? Heal her. Give the medical personnel the wisdom to treat her.

Chapter 28

Barnabas stood at Locklin's bedside, his eyes on her white face, seeing where the blood had not yet been washed away. He saw the blueness of her lips. His heart sank as he prayed, petitioning the heaves for Locklin to survive. He did not want to be the one to tell Buckley that his bride had died and that they had no idea where to find him.

Dr. James paused beside Barnabas, his own eyes assessing the young lady in front of him. He had seen the X-rays, the CT scan, and feared for her very life.

"Dr. James? What can you tell me?" Barnabas spoke without looking away from Locklin.

"She is in critical, life-threatening condition, Barnabas. I know you well enough, to be frank with you. I have seen the imaging studies. It's not good. She has what we call a brain bleed. You understand that?"

Barnabas nodded. "I do. So, what are we looking at? We can't find Buckley, to have him talk to you. I'll have to make whatever decision is necessary for him." Barnabas reached to touch Locklin's hand, finding it cold. "So, what are we looking at? Surgery?"

"That is a distinct possibility. This time, her head hit on the other side from her other injury. I understand that she couldn't remember much."

"Not a lot. Buckley told me that she was starting to remember bits and pieces, but not enough to put together much of her life. How long do we wait?"

"I want to wait until morning, repeat the imaging, and then see where we stand. I don't want to transfer her to a larger hospital if I can avoid it. The travel just might be too much for her at present."

Barnabas paled. "It's that bad?"

"It is, Barnabas. It is. Here. This is what I am proposing for treatment." Dr. James walked Barnabas through the treatment options, answered his questions, and then stood watching as Barnabas prayed and then signed the paperwork. "Thank you, son. I know it's a huge responsibility to put on you."

"Other than Buckley, she has no one. Buckley asked if I would consent to stand behind him like this. I can't say no to the fellows."

"We know you can't." Dr. James grew quiet as he assessed Locklin again. "She's about the same. We may need to intubate her at some point if her breathing worsens. I'll talk to you if that's necessary. For now, you can stay with her, if you wish. We'll be moving her upstairs to an ICU bed shortly. And I have the neurologist on call coming in to assess her as well."

"Can you send Breck in, please? I'll need him to talk to everyone for us."

"I can do that." Dr. James stood and watched Barnabas before he walked away, looking for Breck, who was on his feet heading for the exam rooms as soon as he was told to.

"Barnabas?" Breck's voice was quiet as he stopped beside his friend, drawing in a deep breath as he saw Locklin.

"It's bad, Breck. He said life-threatening. She has a brain bleed as he put it. They may need to do surgery." Barnabas turned to face Breck. "If she dies, how do I tell Buckley?"

Breck drew in another deep breath. "Are they planning for the surgery tonight?"

"No. I just wanted you to update everyone for me. I'll be staying here with her for now. They're moving her to ICU shortly." Barnabas' face hardened for a moment. "We need to find these people, Breck. Where do we stand on that?"

"Not where we want to be. Just like her memory, we're getting bits and pieces. It's trying to piece them together that has us frustrated."

"Find whoever it is that you need to help. Bring in whoever it is. I want this solved and solved soon. Buckley doesn't deserve to have his bride lying here on her death bed."

"No. I've already started that process. The fellows are all drawing back from their work and focusing on this. Emma has been in touch. She and Abe were planning on heading this way in the next day or so." Breck was frustrated and angry and knew he had to pray it through to get his perspective back. "I'll go talk to the ladies. They're out there. They sent the fellows back to the building."

"Did they? And are they working away out there?"

"I suspect so. I talked to Dallas earlier. They found the car, but it was wiped clean, plates were pulled, and the VIN was damaged enough that they can't make it out. Whoever it was also pulled any computer chips that might help."

Barnabas stared at him. "An organized group that knows what they need to take. Organized crime?"

"That's what he's saying. It's what we've been feeling all along, given how Locklin's father died."

Barnabas nodded. "Okay, so that's that. Head off, Breck. I'll be in touch."

Chapter 29

Two days later, Breck stood watching as Barnabas paced his office. Locklin was still unconscious but so far, had not had to have the surgery that she had been threatened with. Breck knew that the fellows and the ladies were waiting for Barnabas to show up and give an update.

"Barnabas? You need to get some sleep."

"I know, Breck. I've had some. Dad had an interesting observation that I need to speak with you about. Only I'm not sure how to express what he said."

"Just say it like he did." Breck perched on the corner of the desk. "What did he say?"

Barnabas returned to his desk, sitting in his chair, leaning forward with his elbows planted on the desk blotter. His cheek rested against his clasped hands.

"We were talking this morning, he had dropped in. He was asking how the investigation was going and if Buckley had appeared. When I say no, he then asked how Locklin was. He is very concerned, I must say as he is for all of us here."

"I know he is. What else?"

"He said that Mom had had a thought. If they wanted to get to Locklin, they would take Buckley and hide him somewhere. But running her down as they did, that was deliberate. I agree with Mom. Dad said she then commented that if they were trying to get to her by taking Buckley, they did it all wrong. They would have stopped, threatened her, and then made her life miserable with taunts about him. She doesn't think it's the same group."

"Doesn't think they're the same group?" Breck stared at him. "You know, that's what Bradon and Blair said. Benen agreed. We've been arguing back and forth that it is."

"Two groups. Two different methods. Two different threats. Two different motives." Barnabas sat back in his chair. "I have to agree. It has never made sense to be one."

"No, it hasn't. Buckley made the same sort of comment, late last week. He also wondered if Locklin had been given something when she was hurt that caused the amnesia. I have to talk to Doc yet about that. He's been working so many hours and then they're away right now."

"That they are. I wondered the same thing. The medication she had wasn't what it was supposed to be." Barnabas stood. "Let's go find the fellows. This may move what they're doing along faster."

"Or complicate it further. I would say that the fellow Buckley put down is one group. He was after Locklin, nothing more. The other group would be related to her father. But what if Locklin knows something and has forgotten it?"

"That's what Brendon asked me last night. I think that's probably the case. But we have no way of knowing. And with her belongings all destroyed, whatever she had in proof would be gone." Barnabas pulled the door to the conference room open and stopped. "Abe's here."

"So he is. And all of his fellows and their ladies. It looks as if we have more help than we planned on."

"I'm glad. Abe? What brings you and Emma and everyone else here?"

"Buckley. We want to help find him. And we want to help solve this." Abe stood for a moment, surveying the room. When he spoke again, only Barnabas could hear him. "I don't think you understand that Buckley has been in touch with each one of my fellows and their ladies every single week since he met them. He talks with them, prays with them. Teases and torments them as Emma would say. They want to help."

"No, I didn't know that, but he does the same here. He thinks differently than the rest of us do."

"He does. He has a servant's heart. He models Christianity in a way that I have seen few do. Maybe, just maybe, he was kidnapped to do that to the group after Locklin." Abe shot Barnabas a look. "How is she?"

"Still unconscious. The physicians are not ruling out surgery yet to relieve the pressure. But if the imaging continues the same or improves, they won't have to. That is how we are all praying."

"As are we. Listen, can we go somewhere and talk? I have some information that I want to run by you before I talk to your men and mine."

"Sure. My office works. Amy is there but if the door is closed, she doesn't interrupt." Barnabas settled Abe down in a chair in front of his desk, mug of coffee handed to him. "It seems that all we do is drink coffee."

Abe grinned. "I know that feeling. Now, about Locklin? Had she remembered anything?"

"Not a lot. Buckley said that she was starting to. She would come out with something about her life or what had happened without thinking. If she was stopped or questioned, she would just look at us and wilt, unable to remember any more details."

"That's what I thought you would say. Now, how do the physicians think this will affect her memory?"

"They have no idea." Barnabas studied his friend. "But that's not what you want."

"No, it's not. Joseph and Luke were doing some research on her home area. I know that the provincial force has authority there. But they have discovered a secret group that runs the area, does their own policing, and keeps people in line. They have ties to a drug lord in South America."

"South America? Drugs? Her father was testifying in court against a drug dealer."

"And he was killed to keep him quiet. We've discovered that. What we have also discovered is who the leader in the area is. It's someone you would least expect."

"That's what Mom said. Who?" Barnabas paled as Abe said the name and occupation. "Him? That really changes it, doesn't it? She would have trusted him completely. Buckley did say that she didn't have many friends or trust too many people. That much she could remember."

"And he would have played that with both her father and herself. We've been tracking him. He's moving back and forth between her area and here."

"That doesn't help, Abe. Now, what? With your experience in security, how do we keep her safe, and then find Buckley?" Barnabas stared at his friend, not sure on where this was taking them.

Chapter 30

Her head moving restlessly, Locklin's hand found the sore spot. Her eyes flickered open and then shut against the brightness of the lights. She sighed. Now, what did he do to me? Lord, I am so tired of him. I want to move on but he won't let me.

Dr. James watched her movements before he reached to assess her eye movements, earning himself a frown before Locklin drifted off again. He reached to flick on the computer monitor near the bed and signed in to view the images that had been taken that morning. He frowned himself. This can't be right, he thought. He verified that they were the images taken that very morning and that they did indeed belong to Locklin. He shook his head.

"I don't understand. It is like she had no injury at all. But I know she did. I saw the evidence." He stepped back, after exiting the program, and watched her. "She's dropping into a natural sleep, isn't she now?"

Barnabas had hesitated as he approached. He would rather it be Buckley that was here, but to date, four days after he seemed to have vanished into thin air, they had not yet found him. He was worried that he would make the wrong decision for Locklin and then have to explain to Buckley why she died.

"Dr. James?" Barnabas spoke quietly.

"Barnabas. Just how much have the people been praying for this young lady?" Dr. James watched him intently.

"Every hour of every day. For both Locklin and Buckley. Why? Is she worse?" Barnabas was almost afraid to hear the answer.

"No, it's the opposite. There is now no evidence of any brain injury. And she had roused." Dr. James peered at him intently. "That's your God at work?"

"It is." Barnabas drew a breath of relief. "Sometimes, this is how He works. Complete healing. Are you saying that she is going to be all right?"

"I would suspect so. We'll have to wait until she fully rouses and then assess her completely. But right now? I would say that it's as if she has never been injured. Even the other injury on the other side of her head that we saw some residual from is gone." He turned to walk away. "Now, just find Buckley and bring him home. I'll be in your church Sunday morning. I want to hear him preach."

Barnabas stared after the physician as he left. Dr. James was known for doubting any divine intervention. As he put it, that was a bunch of garbage. He turned to stare back at Locklin, his mind racing as to why God had allowed this. Finally walking away from the room, he sat in the waiting area, not sure where to go or even who to talk to. The fellows and ladies of the building were deep in either the investigation or their employment.

Berneen found him, Cadee in tow, and paused, not sure if she should approach him. The two ladies shared a look. Barnabas, hearing their footsteps, looked up and then stood, surprising them by hugging both of them.

"Barnabas? Don't tell us!" Berneen blinked back tears.

"It's okay." He smiled, the first genuine smile in a few days, he thought. "She's better."

"Better? How can that be?" Cadee was puzzled. "I thought that she was still critical."

"Last night, she was. I just spoke with Dr. James. God has been good. She's healed. Dr. James just told me that." Barnabas blinked rapidly. "And he is starting to believe. He said he'd be in church on Sunday."

"He will? Wonderful." Berneen looked around. "Is it okay if we go in?"

"I would assume so." Barnabas stepped to where he could see Locklin's room. "Go on. I need to call the fellows and let them know."

Breck paused as he walked through the conference room, stunned at the words he heard. Silence greeted him as all the men stared at him as his eyes slid closed and he couldn't speak. The men exchanges glances, sorrow in them, as they waited for Breck to speak.

Breck had trouble speaking, blinking rapidly to clear his vision. Burnie approached him, a hand resting on his shoulder.

"Breck? When?"

"What?"

"When did she go?"

"She didn't." Breck waited for the murmurs to cease. "Dr. James told Barnabas that she is completely healed. That he would be in church on Sunday and that we needed to find Buckley. He wants to hear him."

The men sat in stunned silence before they broke into cheers and praises.

"He said that? He's known to shun anything like that." Brady stared down at his notes. "That is amazing."

"God is at work. Maybe that's why Locklin was hurt." Blair stood, heading for the door. "I'm finding the ladies. They need to hear this."

Breck nodded, missing Buckley greatly at this time. He should be here, Lord. He would be the one leading us off in a prayer of thanks. I don't know where he is, but You do.

Chapter 31

A day later, Locklin moved slowly through the apartment, not really recognizing anything. She stared at her wedding band and her engagement ring, knowing that she was married, but not really believing it. Where is my husband, she thought. They said he's missing. That he had been missing since I was hurt. And hurt the second time. That doesn't make a lot of sense. I don't remember him.

Locklin reached for a photo that sat on the mantle of the gas fireplace, a finger tracing the face of the man in it. This is Buckley. And me. I wish I could remember him, Lord, but I just don't. And they tell me that I couldn't remember my life from before. I am just so confused. I need healing, Lord, but I can hear a man praying for me, praying that we will both learn to pray. Was that Buckley?

A knock at the door disturbed her thoughts and she moved that way, holding the door partly closed as she stared at the three young ladies, around her age, she thought, who stood there.

"Locklin? I am told that you don't remember us. I'm Cadee. This is Hagen. And this is Fynn. May we come in? If you don't feel like company, that's okay. We'll just leave what we have for you and go on our way."

Locklin finally nodded, standing back to let them in. "I guess, the kitchen? I'm not sure."

———

Fynn grinned at her. "That's okay, Locklin. We understand how strange this is for you. We've all had our troubles, not quite like you, though. Here, can I put this food in your fridge?" She waited for a nod and then did just that.

"Now, what can we do for you?" Cadee watched Locklin closely. "What can we tell you about what has happened?"

"Everything." Locklin dropped into a chair, pointing to the others. "Oh, I'm sorry. I should have offered you coffee or tea." Her brow wrinkled. "I'm not used to company."

"You will be. We drop in and out on one another. There are eleven of us ladies, plus Anna, Doc's wife, and Hagen's twin sisters. You'll be tired of us all." Hagen moved to make the coffee and tea. "I hope you don't mind, but Buckley would say just to go ahead."

"No, that's fine." Locklin looked around. "I just feel so disoriented. I can remember my own apartment. It was so tiny, just a bachelor one. And rough at that. I had hardly anything."

"That's sad, Locklin." Cadee reached for her hand. "May I pray with you?"

"Of course."

After the ladies had left, Locklin still sat at the kitchen table, her finger rubbing along the edge of it. She was disoriented, she thought, and needed to talk to someone who knew her. But she was afraid to do that. Dallas had spoken with her that morning, finding time in his busy day to do that. He had not been able to tell her much about who had run her down, but he had cautioned her to be extremely careful. In his words, he didn't think whoever it had been was done with her yet.

That scared her. She rose, almost running through the apartment, hearing a phone ringing and not finding it. She paused, frowning. There, it was ringing again. She searching, finally pulling it from under a cushion on the living room couch. Locklin stared down at it, before she touched the screen, to waken it.

Her hand covered her mouth as she stared down at the photo. Buckley? But where was he? What had happened to him? She crumpled to the floor, sobs shaking her body as she mourned for him. In her mind, he was dead. Reaching again for the phone, she studied the photo and then say the text that went with it.

She was not ready to meet with anyone, that much she knew. But if she didn't, would Buckley remain alive? Who could she talk to?

Grabbing her keys and locking the door after her, she slowly walked down the stairs, to stand in the lobby, searching for someone, anyone, who could help her. Seeing no one, she dropped into a chair, drawing up her legs and burying her face against them.

Blair and Brennen paused as they moved by her, sharing a look, before they walked towards her. Blair crouched down beside her, a hand on her arm, causing her to jump.

"Locklin? What happened?" He stared down at the phone that she kept thrusting at him. "Your phone? What about it?"

"Buckley. There's a photo. I think he's dead. They sent a picture and a text message."

"Who did?"

"I don't know. They're sending me messages. I can't read them." She looked up at them. "Make them stop."

Brennen studied her before he reached for the phone. "May I?" At her nod, he scrolled through her messages. "I don't see any voice mail. Some of these have come from Buckley's phone. Some from a blocked number. Locklin, I'm taking your phone and giving it to Dallas. Don't worry, we'll find you another one."

"Buckley said no one should have that number. How?"

"From his phone, more than likely." Brennen stood watching her. "Locklin? Are you going to be okay on your own? You've just come home and it must be hard to be on your own."

Locklin shrugged. "I guess. It's what I've been used to for the last while. I miss my dad." She blinked rapidly before she was on her feet. "Fynn said that you were all working on this. How can I help?"

"Right now, we need you to finish healing." Blair watched her closely, seeing the fatigue in her face.

"I can't. Not when this is going on. Where do we start?"

"For tonight, you rest. We'll come to find you in the morning. After 9. Not a moment before." Brennen had returned with a phone for her. "Our numbers are in there. Call us if you need anything, even just to talk. Buckley is always there for us. We can do no difference for the one he loves."

"He loves me? How can that be?" Locklin was shocked at the thought.

"He told me that when he saw you running towards him and he stepped in, that he knew he had found his lady. His love for you had just grown day by day. Those are his words." Blair escorted her back to her apartment and waited for her to enter before he walked through it. "It's good, Locklin. And we mean that you call us if you need us."

Locklin closed and locked the door, heading for the living room. She curled up on the couch, a blanket over her, not willing to settle into any of the bedrooms. She didn't think that she would sleep, but her fatigue and injury had other ideas. She slept, her sleep full of dreams of Buckley.

Chapter 32

Breck ran for his truck, his phone to his ear. He could only faintly hear sounds, but he recognized one of the voices. Buckley! Now, to find out where he was! Driving away rapidly, he headed for town, looking for Dallas.

His phone in his hand, he approached Dallas as he stood in the line at the coffee shop.

"Dallas? It's Buckley!"

"What?" Dallas grabbed his coffee and sandwich with a quick thank you. "What are you talking about?"

"Here. On my phone. It's his phone that I'm hearing. I can hear him but I can also hear others. I just don't know where they are."

Dallas took the phone and then sent the link on to the techs. "I'm hoping that they can trace this. Here, follow me. We'll head back in and see what they can say." He paused, his cup of coffee on the roof of his car, as his phone rang. "What's that? You have a location already? Oh, it was reported to you? Okay. Let me have it. Patrol on the way?" He pointed at Breck as he caught up his cup of coffee. "In. You're coming with me." He tossed Breck back his phone.

"Dallas? What is going on?" Breck barely was seated before Dallas had taken off, driving as rapidly as the traffic would allow, finally moving at a higher rate of speed as he hit the highway.

"We have the address that call came from. Patrol had been out there earlier, following up complaints of noise and gunfire. They had pulled up as close as they could and are watching the building." Dallas shot a look towards Breck. "It's near the old Smothers' place."

"The Smothers' place? As in Brody and Ker and that Smothers?"

"Exactly." Dallas slowed his vehicle as he made a sharp right turn, Breck grabbing for something to hold on to. "We'll get you back to your truck. Right now, check your phone."

Breck did just that. "Nothing more. That was so bizarre." He stared down at a text message. "Locklin is looking for me. She's worried. And now Fynn. She's with Locklin. Says Locklin is frantic with worry about Buckley."

"I thought that she really didn't remember me." Dallas' eyes narrowed against the sun as he slowed and then parked behind the patrol vehicle, his window lowering as the officer approached. "What do we have?"

"A lot of traffic has been going in and out from the other side. I took a walk around, keeping in the shadows. A number of known drug dealers for starters." The office peered at Breck. "Breck?"

"We traced Buckley's phone to here." Dallas watched the building.

"That makes sick sense, you know. Buckley is so anti-drug. Put him in here. Not necessarily get him stoned, but let the smell of the drugs permeate his clothing. Where would that put him with the church?"

"Exactly. Keep an eye on the traffic. I need to call Will and make some plans."

Two hours later, Breck stood back, watching as the various squads moved in towards the house. He jerked as he heard gunfire and then the shouts of the authorities. He paced away, his phone out, knowing that he needed to check in with the fellows but not sure what to say.

"Barnabas?"

"Breck? Where are you? Brady found your truck, but not you. You've worried us." Barnabas paused as he heard the faint noise. "Breck? What is going on?"

"I got a call from Buckley's phone, took off to find Dallas. Right now, I standing watching as they move into a drug house. We tracked Buckley to here."

"You did? I guess you can't say much. Call me when you can." Barnabas cut off the call, rising from his desk and heading for the chapel. He knew that was where the fellows had gathered along with the ladies. He paused in the doorway, hearing the prayers, and just waiting until they were finished.

They all looked up at him as he walked to the front of the chapel and then turned, rubbing at his cheek.

"People? Breck received a call this morning from Buckley's phone. He tracked down Dallas. Right now, the police are moving in on a location where they think he is."

"And they can't tell us where." Brandon was frustrated. "All we can do is pray. I, for one, am heading back to my research." He was on his feet and out of the room, the door swinging closed behind him.

Quiet conversation filtered around the room before the men all rose and walked back to the conference room. They were determined to find Buckley and in finding him, bring to justice those responsible.

Barnabas watched as the ladies gathered around Locklin before he approached her.

"Locklin?"

His quiet voice startled her and she stared at him, fear on her face.

"I'm sorry. I didn't mean to startle you. What can we do for you?"

She shrugged. "I don't know. Everyone is always asking me that. I have no idea."

"Then, we do what we can for you. For now, the ladies are with you. If you need anything, find one of us." Barnabas walked away, knowing that he had a number of calls to make, but they would wait while he spent time in prayer. One of those calls would be to his parents.

Locklin watched him leave, before she too rose, walking away from the ladies, not even aware that she had not excused herself. She settled into a chair in the lobby, her focus on the door. She was expecting God to answer her prayer and that Buckley would walk through that very door that day.

———

Chapter 33

Searching through the rooms in the dilapidated building, his weapon at the ready, Dallas followed after the Emergency Response Team members. He heard the shouts and scattered gunfire from the men around him, but his focus was on finding Buckley. He heard a sharp cry and spun, heading for the small room next to him. He searched the room before his eyes fell on the huddled, tumbled mass of blankets, an officer on his knees beside it.

"Joe?"

"It's Buckley. He's unconscious."

Dallas was on his knees as well, pulling back the blankets and the broken down cardboard cartons that partially covered him. "Is he alive?"

"He is. He's not drugged. At least, I don't think so but he's hurt."

"Here. Let's get him up." Dallas' weapon was back in its holster. "Over my shoulders. Which is the quickest, clearest way out?"

"This way." Joe led him out, watching carefully.

Dallas moved as quickly as he could towards the waiting ambulance, handing Buckley off to the paramedics before he stood back, a dark look on his face. "Joe? You were paired with someone?"

"I was. I'll ride with him."

Breck watched anxiously as the ambulance moved past him. He had heard the sounds of activity around it but had not been able to see much. He looked up to see Dallas walking towards him.

"Breck? In the car." Dallas merely pointed at his vehicle. "We're heading into the hospital."

"Buckley?" Breck fastened his seatbelt, ready for another wild ride.

"We gave him, Breck. He's unconscious. We'll find out more when we get there." Dallas shifted on his seat, fatigue setting in as it always did after a raid like that one. "There's a lot of work to do, but right now, Buckley is my focus."

Breck held up his phone. "Can I call?"

Dallas nodded. "Just have Barnabas bring Locklin in. I don't know what to tell her."

"Simply that Buckley is alive and receiving help." Breck's attention shifted as he heard Barnabas answer. "Barnabas?"

"Breck? Where are you now?" Barnabas had tracked down Locklin and was sitting watching her, the fellows and the ladies gathered around. None of them wanted to or were willing to leave her.

"Barnabas? Where's Locklin?"

Barnabas' heart fell. "Right here. Breck?"

"Bring her to the hospital, Barnabas."

Barnabas was on his feet, his hand on Locklin's arm as she looked up, fear briefly showing on her face.

"Breck?"

"We have him, Barnabas. We have Buckley."

Barnabas' eyes slid closed in relief. "He's alive?"

"He is. Dallas said he's out of it. We need Locklin."

"On our way." Barnabas' phone was away as he crouched down beside Locklin, knowing the others were moving closer. "Locklin? We have him."

Locklin stared at him, not quite sure of what he had said. "What?"

"We have Buckley. We'll need to go to the hospital, but he's alive. I'll take you to him."

Locklin sat still, unable to move, before she was on her feet, moving towards the door, belying the fatigue and pain that she was feeling. Even though the surgeon had released her, he had warned her about overdoing it. That was exactly what she had done.

The fellows and ladies scattered, moving towards the parking area, sorting themselves out into vehicles. Barnabas tucked Locklin into his truck, and then drove away, a slight smile on his face as he saw the caravan following him. He knew that he would need to call Charles, but for now, Locklin was his priority, and that priority was to get her back with Buckley.

Chapter 34

Locklin shifted from foot to foot, unsure of herself where Buckley was concerned, but anxious to meet him in person. She had remembered most of what had happened, but she felt that he was a stranger once more. That bothered her, and she had to pray for forgiveness, she thought, and then for strength and wisdom.

Blair moved with her as she entered the exam room. He had volunteered and she had accepted that. She knew the others were waiting. Doc looked around as she came towards him, his keen eyes on her white face.

"Locklin? He's right here. There, you stand right beside him." Doc moved her to the position he wanted her in. Buckley had been rousing and Doc wanted Locklin to be the first one that he saw.

"Doc?" Blair's voice held the question that he knew Locklin couldn't or wouldn't ask.

"No drugs. Not that we can tell. That's an answer to prayer. He's been ill-used, to say the least. He's starting to rouse, Locklin. I want you where he can see you. The nurses have been around, cleaned him up some. We're running bloodwork to see what is happening."

"Any X-Rays or anything, Doc?" Blair's voice startled Locklin, who had forgotten that he was there.

"Not unless we feel there is a need. So far, we don't see that." Doc stepped back. "I'll find Barnabas, if you like, Locklin."

She shrugged. "I don't care." She missed the looks that the men shared.

Doc watched as the building folks, as he called them, milled around, inside and outside. He shook his head. The family just keeps growing, doesn't it, Lord? Gives me more to pray for, but more to share with. He walked towards Barnabas, who headed his way.

"Doc?"

"I'll take you back to Locklin. Now that she's here, I have to speak with her." Doc looked apologetic.

"I understand. Just one thing, so I can tell the others. He's okay?"

"Seems to be." Doc could hear the breath of relief that wafted from person to person. "Come. Blair's with her, but he needs to be with Devaney."

"I know. They will all want to see him."

"And they can't. I'll put restrictions on him for now. I have to until Dallas or someone can take his statement. It is enough that you and Locklin are here with him." Doc pointed at Blair. "You can leave, but don't say anything."

"I won't, Doc." Blair grinned at Doc's pretended gruffness. "I'll leave it for Locklin."

Barnabas studied Locklin and then turned his attention to Buckley, shock momentarily stopping him in his tracks.

"Doc?"

"I know. He looks rough. That unkempt beard and hair don't help. Stay here for now. We'll move him to a room, if we can, when one becomes available. And those are in extremely short supply today. Everyone in town seems to think that they need to be in the hospital overnight." Doc grumbled away, knowing that Barnabas took it in the spirit he meant it.

"Locklin?"

Locklin looked around at Doc. "Doc? What's wrong with him?"

"Likely malnourishment. Dehydration. Hypothermia. It's been chilly overnight lately, and I doubt he had the heat and covers that he needed." Doc reached to draw her to him, just as he would his own daughter. "He'll make it, Locklin. You both will. God had provided for you. He's brought Buckley back. Why you two have had to go through this, we may never know. If you hadn't, Dr. James, for one, would not be willing to learn about God."

"That's true. I had some talks with him before I left the hospital. He is seeking."

"He is." Doc paused as he saw Buckley moving. "Now, young lady, your fellow is waking up. He doesn't want to see my old face. He wants to see you." Doc moved her closer to the head of the bed and then stepped away. "I'll be back."

Dallas hesitated at the doorway, knowing that he had to talk to Buckley, but not wanting to interrupt. His duties finally won and he walked forward, just as Buckley discovered Locklin standing beside him.

"Locklin? You're here? Thank you! They told me that they had done the same to you as they had your father."

Chapter 35

Buckley's hand reached for Locklin and then he withdrew it, seeing the marks and dirt streaking it. Locklin simply reached to take it, her eyes on him, a puzzled frown on her face.

"Locklin, I was so worried. I thought you were dead."

"No, I'm not. But you were gone for what seemed forever. Doc said that they might keep you in." She really wasn't sure what to say to him, now that he was in front of her. All the sentences and words that she had planned to say just flew from her mind.

Buckley looked past her at Dallas. "Dallas? You'll want to talk to me. I'm not letting Locklin leave. And Barnabas? You're here? Where is everyone else?"

"Hanging around the building somewhere. We missed you." Barnabas stepped back, not wanting to intrude on Dallas' questions.

Dallas nodded. "We need to talk, Buckley, but I'll wait for a bit. Just give the basics."

"I didn't see who it was. And I can't remember much of it. Does that help?"

"Not a whole lot. I'll talk to you in a bit. I need to speak with Doc first. Barnabas?"

"With you." The men walked away, Locklin turning to watch them.

"Locklin, love. Are you okay?"

"No, I'm not. I'm not sure of anything anymore."

"Something has changed with you." Buckley reached to raise the head of the bed. "What happened?"

"I was run down, had a brain bleed, spent I don't know how long in a coma, woke up, remembered who I was, and forgot who you were. Isn't that enough?" She struggled to contain her tears and couldn't.

Buckley made an inaudible sound and then swung off the bed, gathering her close to him, his heart breaking as she sobbed. Why, Lord? Why us? Why Locklin? She didn't deserve any of this. I know, Lord, I'm questioning and I shouldn't. But I'm human and I'm a husband with a hurting wife.

"Love? Can you talk to me?"

Locklin shook her head. "I don't know where to start. I'm scared, Buckley. Scared of so much." She sniffed and then swiped at her face. "I am scared to be on my own. And I just know I will be."

"I'm not letting you go. That's what they wanted. They wanted me to give up on you. To let you walk away from me. They planned to take you. They were plotting revenge against you and your father."

"That's what the fellows have said. I don't know why. I didn't know what Dad was up to." She leaned against him. "You shouldn't be on your feet."

"I will be if I need to be, and right now, that's what you need. Can you spring me? I want to go home."

"Not until Doc says so. And Dallas is wanting to talk to you." She stepped back as Buckley reached for her hand. "Buckley, we can't leave."

"We can. I know, it's against medical advice, but I can't be in a small room. Not tonight. I need space." He looked both ways in the corridor and then headed away from the waiting room, towards the bays where the ambulances offloaded their stretchers. "Out this way. One of the fellows will be watching for me."

"And just how would they know that?" She was shocked that he would leave like that.

"Because it's what I do. I come in and out this way all the time." He pointed. "There. Benen and Cadee are watching for us. Quick. Into their truck." Buckley shoved her in, jumped in after her, and slammed the door, a grin on his face. "Home, James."

"James? Memory failing you, Buckley? No offense, Locklin." Benen just grinned at him. "Didn't get your discharge, I take it?"

"Nope. I'll talk to Doc later. Right now, I just want to go home, get cleaned up, and have a decent meal. As well as spending time with my love." His arm went around Locklin. "Benen. Cadee. Thank you. And which one of you won the bet?"

"Cadee. She said you'd be coming out in ten minutes from when Barnabas appeared back in the waiting room. I thought twenty."

Cadee grinned. "I know our minister. He doesn't hang around when he needs to be somewhere else. I sent out a group text. They'll head for home. They will all want to see you."

"I know. Can it wait until tomorrow? Dallas will have tracked me down by then." Fatigue was setting in. Buckley yawned, his arm around Locklin, content for the moment.

Chapter 36

Late that night, Buckley paced his office. He had had a chance to clean up, trim his beard, and let Locklin trim his hair as best she could. She had frowned at him as he had grinned when making his request. He was puzzled. Something had changed with her, and he was just quite sure what. He still had to talk to her, to find out what all happened in the days that he had been gone.

Dallas had appeared a few hours prior, staring at Buckley before shaking his head.

"You just had to, didn't you?" He dropped his laptop onto the kitchen table and then headed to dish up a plate of food offered to him. He hadn't had a chance to have his dinner and this was welcome.

Buckley had grinned. "Of course. Doc called Locklin. He wasn't surprised."

"No, that what he said. Now, I need to talk to you, to find out what exactly happened." Dallas looked up as Locklin left. "Did she just leave?"

"She did. I'll talk to her. Now, what is it that you want to hear?" Buckley knew that Locklin had stopped just outside the kitchen doorway. Her footsteps had not gone much past there.

"Tell me what happened. I know that you wouldn't in front of Doc or Barnabas." Dallas wiped his hands on the napkin that he had been given and brought up his word processing program on his laptop. "You've been through this before, only not as the victim."

Buckley's hand paused as he rubbed it on the tabletop. "That's what I am, isn't it? A victim? A victim of crime. I have often counselled those very victims. I never expected to be one myself."

"But you have been in the past. With Baird and Berneen." Dallas watched him closely, seeing the fatigue in his friend's face. "Let's get started, Buckley. Doc gave me strict instructions to tell you that you were to rest. And that he would be around later tonight or early tomorrow morning."

"I am sure that he will be." Buckley hesitated, a prayer rising from within him, knowing that he could give few details. "I'm not sure what is going on. Something involving Locklin. But there seems to be more than one involved."

Buckley began by giving his full name and the date before he began to speak.

He had just walked down the steps at the church and towards his car when he was tackled and then shoved into a vehicle. A blindfold had been slapped around his eyes and his wrists bound behind him. Shoved to the floor in the backseat of the car, he had felt a foot resting on his back. Drawing in his breath, he wasn't sure what was going on. He just prayed for safety and for protection for his beloved Locklin.

Buckley had felt the car driving around for what appeared to be hours, and he was sure that they were just driving in circles, although he could feel the different speeds and sounds of country and town hitting at his ears.

He had finally been pulled from the vehicle and shoved towards a building, stumbling as he struggled to keep his feet. A hand was bunched in the back of his shirt, the brutal manner of that scaring him. And Buckley knew that few things scared him. This did. This unknown of what he was facing scared him. And all he could do was pray. And even that was difficult.

The door slammed behind him as he rested on his hands and knees. A violent push had sent him through the doorway and to that position. He could feel the nicks on his wrists where the knife had slashed at his bounds. Buckley finally rose, pulling off the blindfold, and staring around. A ramshackle room, he thought, trying to wrap his mind around the fact that he had been kidnapped. The fading sunlight barely made a dent in the dimness of the room, the window was that streaked with dust and mud and dirt.

Buckley sank back down to the floor in the middle of the room, staring around at the debris that littered it. Broken cardboard cartons, broken bottles, wine and beer, he thought, crushed plastic bottles, other garbage. Then, his gaze centred on the debris in the corner, and his eyes slid shut. A drug house, he thought. They've brought me into a drug house. Even against my will and as a prisoner, how do I explain that to my church?

Days passed. Buckley saw no one, received no food or water. He began to grow weak, his prayers the only thing that kept him sane, that and his quoting of the Bible verses that he had memorized over the years and the hymns and choruses that he could sing. He wasn't aware that when he slept, one of his captors would stand over him, just watching.

His captors had been given strict instructions. Buckley was to be left alone, no contact with them. They were only to approach him when he was sleeping. The men had looked at one another and then shrugged. They didn't know who was giving the orders but they were being paid good money to follow those very instructions.

On the last night, Buckley had roused as he heard the door open and the man approached him. He was on his feet, his hands in fists at his sides, as he demanded answers, answers that he didn't receive. He had charged at the man, desperate to escape, only to fall to the dirt and debris-covered floor, blood trickling from the cut on his head, a cruel blow from the wooden bat that the man held.

Buckley had been unaware the next morning as he had been roused, that he had dialled Breck's number and then tucked his phone under some of the debris. He had protested that he didn't know what they wanted and why him, anyway? He was a minister, a pastor, a servant. He didn't have contacts on the wrong side of the track. He had dropped once more from the blows across his face, his head hitting in a sodden manner on the floor, before he lay still.

Chapter 37

Unaware that Breck had received his call and gone for help, Buckley had not moved from where he had fallen. He didn't hear the shouts and gunfire in the dilapidated house or hear the running footsteps. He didn't hear the door broken down and the cries for help when he was discovered, covered as he was with tangled blankets and garbage hastily kicked over him.

Dallas had approached and then dropped beside him, joining the officer who had found him, before they had him on his feet and draped over Dallas' shoulder, moved rapidly from the house and then to the waiting ambulance. Buckley had not felt the hands that assessed him. He was unaware of the race to the hospital or Doc standing staring down at him. He had been unaware of anything until he finally roused and found Locklin standing beside him.

Buckley looked up at last. "I'm sorry, Dallas. I can't tell you much. I was too out of it and it was too dark to be able to see what the man looked like."

"We get that, Buckley." Dallas read back through what little Buckley had been able to tell him. "You really don't have much of a statement. Here. I'll print it off, have you sign it, and then take it in. I'll have another detective go over it and then talk to you again, just so they can't say anything, seeing as I was the one to find you."

"I never thought of that, you know. That's a possibility." Buckley sat back. "Is that all?"

"It is. I know you won't say much, but that house was a drug house, just as you thought. We've made arrests, including the men who have admitted kidnapping you. But they don't know who they are working for."

"I see." Buckley's attention was on the far wall, not seeing how Dallas was watching him. "Now what, Dallas? How do we find them?"

"We work on it. We need you fellows to pull back. These are dangerous people that are involved in this." Dallas watched him and then sighed. "And I know that you won't pull back. Not one of you will. Just stay safe."

"We will. Doc muttered something about Dr. James hearing me preach. What was with that?" He turned as Locklin appeared beside him, and simply wrapped an arm around her to draw her down on his knee. "Locklin?"

"He treated me, Buckley. When I was healed without any medical intervention, he asked Barnabas if it was God, in words something like that, and then said that we had to find you. That he would be in church on Sunday and that he wanted to hear you preach."

"Dr. James? Wow! God is at work in all this."

"He is, Buckley. No matter how dark or how dangerous, He is at work." Dallas stood, gathering his

———

belongings and then walking away, the door closing softly behind him.

Locklin stood at long last, her eyes on Buckley, before she reached to clear the dishes and set the food away. He watched her, a frown on his face. Something has changed, he thought, and I don't know what.

"Locklin? What happened?"

Locklin hesitated before she turned. "What do you mean?"

"I mean. What happened to you? You seem different."

"I guess that I am. I was run down in the parking lot here. I was in a coma for a bit, with a brain bleed. They thought I would have to have surgery, but God intervened and healed me. I have remembered my past, Buckley, and the last year or so is not pretty. I'll pack and be gone in the morning."

Buckley sat in stunned silence, staring at the spot where Locklin had just stood before he was on his feet and following her. A hand on her bedroom door braced him on his feet.

"Locklin? Just like that? You walk away without talking it over with me? Without giving me a chance to say yes or no?"

Locklin refused to look at him. "It's for the best. I brought this trouble to you. I don't want you to be hurt anymore. Or have anyone else hurt."

Buckley moved towards her, his hands raised to touch her, opening and closing before he reached to turn her towards him and then sweep her to him, his hug tight. He felt her stiffen and then her arms wrapped around him, her tears soaking into his shirt, his soaking in the red hair that he had dreamed about when he was away from her.

"I can't let you go, love. You would take my heart with you if you did. Please? Don't walk away from me."

"I don't want you to be hurt." Locklin repeated herself. "I couldn't live with myself if they killed you."

"God is in control, love. He is in control. We need to trust Him."

"And that's so hard. I am learning all over again how hard. And to pray, Buckley." She leaned back, her eyes clouded with her tears. "We'll talk. I promise that I would leave without letting you know. But for now, you need to seek your rest. Doc made me promise that when he called a bit ago."

"Checking up on me?" Buckley grinned before his head lowered and he kissed her. "That's a promise, love. I love you so much. You're my Proverbs 31 lady."

She frowned at him for a moment. "Buckley? It's Friday. You have to preach on Sunday, don't you?"

He grinned again as he shrugged. "I suppose I must. But it's okay, love. We'll figure it out." He kissed her again, reluctant to let her go, before he walked away, closing her door softly behind him, to stand with his head back against it, fear in his heart that she would do exactly what she had said, walk away from him.

Locklin stared at the closed door, her fingers on her lips, a softened look on her face. No, she thought, I just can't, Lord. Please help me. I just can't walk away from him, and I should. She felt peace in her heart, knowing that to stay with Buckley was exactly where God wanted her. She frowned for a moment. She didn't know anything about being a minister's wife, now did she? She felt ill-fitted to do that. She only had a high school education, not having the money to go on to college or university. And even if she had, she wouldn't have known what to study.

Chapter 38

Walking around the conference room the next morning, Locklin's hand tight in his, Buckley studied what his friends had discovered. He was not surprised at how many details had been added to the boards that now lined the walls, taking the place of the paper that had been there. Whose idea is that, he wondered?

Locklin paused as a board, her finger tracing her father's name, before she read what was there. There were details that she had not known about her father. He had been reluctant to talk about his family, and now she knew why. They were involved, his cousins, ones that she never had heard about. She then turned to the board that held the information for Buckley's family.

"I didn't realize that you were here for such a short time. I thought this was your home area."

Buckley's arm around her, he shook his head. "No, Just about eight or nine years. For all intents and purposes, it is my home. I won't leave it, not unless God wills."

"I pray that He doesn't, but I know that's not right."

"No, it's not. We have to trust Him, no matter how hard." He turned as he heard the door.

The fellows had gathered for prayer in the chapel before heading to the conference room, stopping in surprise at seeing Buckley already there.

"Buckley! You're here!" Burnie walked towards him, reaching to hug him before he stood back. "You look rough."

"Only you, Burnie, would greet someone that way." Bradon laughed as he reached to shake Buckley's hand and then hug Locklin, to her surprise. "Welcome home. Now, what can you tell us?"

"Bradon! Give him a moment or two to get used to us again." Baird simply shook his head. "Buckley, I agree. What can you tell us?"

Buckley shook his head, seated Locklin at a table, and then proceeded to tell them what he could.

"I don't know a lot more than that. I don't recall seeing enough of any of the men to give any descriptions." He looked around. "Thank you, all of you, for praying for me and for taking care of Locklin. She won't say, but I know that you all did just that."

"Okay, so where do we go?" Benen rose and walked to the empty board. "Buckley? What was your sense of where you were? Dallas isn't saying."

"In a drug house. I would say around the edge of town somewhere. I know they drove me around for hours, in and out of town, but it seemed aimless. I didn't get much of a sense other than that."

"Okay, so they drove you around. Why?"

"Waiting for dark. Waiting for orders. To terrorize him. To get to Locklin." Brady spoke from where he stood near the door. "They would want him to be frightened for her. Did they say anything about her?"

Buckley had to think about that one. "No, they didn't. I'm surprised. When I asked them why, they simply said that they were told to hold me and that I had to cooperate with them." He was puzzled. "I'm not sure why. They didn't give any names or any reason."

"That doesn't surprise me." Breck had appeared in the room. "You weren't that far away from here, Buckley. Security has had numerous hits on the system, picking up men wandering around the building and gardens at night. We suspect they are trying to find a way into so that they can get to Locklin."

"Her father?" Buckley shared a look with Locklin.

"That's the supposition, but we have to prove that or have Dallas and his fellow officers do that. And the ladies are on a race to beat us in solving this."

"That they are." Brendon spoke distractedly, his eyes on what he was reading. He looked up at Locklin. "Locklin, do you know a Tommy Hall?"

"No, should I?"

"He's from your area, but younger than you. He's been a suspect in a lot of drug dealing in that area and then moving outwards, towards here."

"He is? And just who is he?"

"Brother to the man who was chasing you. They had different names." Brendon watched her closely, see her frown, but not reacting any differently. "Locklin?"

"I'm sorry. I don't know him. That monster didn't live with his family, that much I know. He lived on the streets or whatever abandoned building he could find. He was well known for that. That made him difficult to avoid."

"We understand that. About this man who was chasing you? Have we talked much about him?"

"No, because I couldn't remember. His name is Len Forester. He's older than me but not by much. He had no visible income, not that we could find out. Dad tried to find out for me. I talked to Dad and he helped me to avoid Forester." Locklin felt Buckley's hand tighten on hers. "He was horrible. I think that he was involved in a lot of the crime that went on in the area. I just couldn't prove it."

"He was." Brennen's voice was gentle. "We have proven it, Locklin. Dallas and his team have proved it."

"You have?" Locklin sat back, stunned, before she leaned forward. "Does that mean this is over for me?"

"No, unfortunately, it doesn't. They still have to arrest him. They are working on the charges and hope to do that soon." Brandon approached the board, paper in hand, as he added notes. "We are finding out more and more about his habits and who he hangs around with."

"The lowlife in town and area. That's who." Locklin was on her feet, moving towards the door before she stopped. She didn't look around as her head went back and her face was raised to the ceiling. They watched as her head dropped back down and then she just quietly left, the door closing softly behind her.

Chapter 39

Buckley finally tracked Locklin down that morning, finding her curled up in a chair in the lobby, a mug in her hand. Cadee had been around, just sitting with her, not saying anything. The other ladies had come and gone, their quiet chatter and laughter helping to heal her. She felt out of place, not because they made her feel that way, but just for what she had gone through and what she felt that she had put Buckley through.

Dropping down on the floor beside her, Buckley stretched out his legs, his eyes on the sitting area on the other side of the lobby. He waited, not sure how to approach his bride, knowing that she had remembered her past.

"Buckley? Where do we go from here?" Locklin's question was not unexpected.

"We wait, love. We wait for God to direct our paths. We pray. I have learned more about praying than I ever thought I could. It's a work in progress."

"It is. Dad used to refer to it as a conversation with his best friend. He would talk to God anywhere and everywhere."

"That's how it should be. We complicate it."

"I know. But where do we go? I have a lot of garbage in my past."

"We all do. Garbage of all kinds." He tilted his head to look up at her. "I love you, Locklin."

She stared down at him. "You keep saying that, Buckley." Her voice was very soft. "I know you do. But I'm not lovable."

"But you are, love. You are. He's done this to you, made you feel cheap and unlovable, just by how he's treated you." Buckley was on his feet, his hands drawing her up, and then he was leading her from the lobby, towards the rose garden. "Mom explained something to me one day. She loved her roses. She picked a rosebud and forced it to flower. She said it wouldn't smell the same as a rose that had been allowed to bloom naturally, facing all the forces that nature could throw at it. She was right. The bloom had very little scent. But the ones in the garden? They smelled wonderful. When I smell a rose, I think of her illustration." He looked down at her, finding her gaze intent on him. "You are like the bud that has been allowed to grow naturally, facing all the elements, fighting to survive, and finally bloom. You have something about you that draws people to you."

"But I'm not a minister's wife."

"Don't judge what a minister's wife must be based on what you were raised with. Each lady is unique, just as the minister is unique. Where God has placed you, is right where He wants you. He planned that for you."

"He did? I never thought of it that way." Locklin looked thoughtful before a smile brightened her face. "So, what I have been through, the elements and forces of human nature that I have faced? They have made me who I am and ready to face this?"

"Exactly." Buckley stooped to kiss her. "And made you my help-meet." He hugged her, content to just stand and hold her. "Together, love, we'll get through this. We'll come out victorious. Battered and bruised, with scars more than likely, but together and with God, we'll win."

"I know, Buckley. I know, sweetheart. But it feels like there is no end to the battle." She looked around him as she heard footsteps. "Barnabas?"

"I was looking for you two. Buckley? How are you feeling?" Barnabas pointed to the benches and sat, watching the young couple closely.

"Not quite myself. It will take a bit." He studied his friend. "What is it?"

Barnabas grinned. "You know me too well. Charles has called. The board is concerned that you won't be up to giving a message tomorrow. They would like you to just talk, about whatever, no notes or formatted message. They also plan on a prayer and praise portion."

"They do? I guess he must have tried to call me. I have to get another phone."

"That you do. Breck has one for you. Locklin, your phone is okay? No more messages?"

"No. That stopped. They must have gotten the number from Buckley's phone."

"That's strange, you know. They never took my phone."

"No? They were waiting for you to use it to call for help. I would suspect that if you had, you would not have been found in the condition that you were."

"No, I suspect not. Now, about this investigation? Abe has been involved?" He looked between the two with him as they laughed.

"He has been, Buckley. Abe and Emma and his men and their ladies all showed up here one day to work with our fellows and ladies. They moved it forward a lot. Kataleen had her family tree worked out for both of you."

"That doesn't surprise me. Not one bit." Buckley's attention was drawn back to something Barnabas had said. "You were receiving messages, love?"

"I was. Nasty, horrible ones." Locklin looked up at him. "I hate that they were doing this to us. Trying to drive us apart."

Barnabas made a sound, drawing their attention to him. "What did you just say, Locklin?"

"What part? That they are trying to drive us apart. That's exactly what they are doing." She looked disgruntled. "Why?"

"If it is Forester or his friends, it is because he lost you. If it is Hall and the ones that he works for, he is trying to discredit you and through you to discredit Buckley. Buckley?"

Buckley raised his face, a thoughtful look on it. "That could be it, Barnabas. I don't remember making any enemies, but who is related in the church to the drug dealers that her father was testifying against?"

Barnabas pointed at his friend. "I think that you just broke through the barrier that we were stuck against." His phone was out and he sent off a quick message to Brendon. "Brendon was going that route if I remember correctly. He just wasn't sure if it was correct."

Chapter 40

A week later, Buckley stood in his office, his hand resting on the door frame as he stared out across the Foundation property towards the road. He usually enjoyed the view, but today, he was troubled. Just by what, he couldn't say. He had been back in the church office, out visiting his people, but never on his own. Barnabas had insisted that he have one of the security teams with him from the building. He had been reluctant but one look at Locklin had him acquiescing to the request.

His mind drifted to the past weeks and what his friends had been through. God, I have no idea what is going on. You do. You allow this. Teach us to trust. Teach us to pray, Lord. We need to pray, to have that communication with you.

Locklin's arm slid around him. She was opening back up to him, her love for him declared in words as she became more confident. They just stood, not speaking, not needing to.

"It's Sunday again tomorrow, Buckley."

"It is. I am ready, I think. I'm not sure that the people are."

"And why is that?" Locklin looked up at him, finding him still watching the outside.

"I am planning on starting the series on prayer. With Christ's prayer in the garden. There is so much in that."

"There is. It's one of your favourite passages, isn't it?"

"It is." Buckley turned them away from the door, reaching to close the drapes. "And what have you been up to?"

"I have been with the ladies." She grinned. "We are working on our adventure, as they call it, We have made progress, I think."

"You have? Care to share?"

"After dinner. I have that ready when you are. Just a green salad and grilled chicken. I love all these appliances that you have that I can't put a name to."

"You do, do you? I make up placards and place them around for you." He ducked the elbow that she playfully shot at him.

Later that evening, Locklin snuggled down against Buckley, content, even though she knew that the dangerous part of what they faced was approaching. Everyone had warned her of that fact.

"What did you ladies discover?" Buckley finally broke the stillness.

"That Lois is in fact not related to me. She thought she was but Mom never had a sister or a female cousin. So, why did she say that? I asked Cadee. She says Lois has always maintained that she had a sister who died in childbirth and that her sister's husband refused contact with her."

"That's strange." Buckley sighed. "So, you ladies researched Lois?"

"We did with some help from Emma. She found that out about Mom. She said it was hard to find, that Mom's history was buried. And she found out who by." Locklin was hesitant to continue.

"Lois?" Buckley groaned as she nodded. "This really complicates everything. Not your fault, love."

"I know. We can't figure out why though. Emma has promised to keep looking into Lois. She says that Lois' family had quite a few numbered companies that don't seem to exist."

"Numbered companies?" Buckley grew silent, the possibilities racing through his mind. "As in crime?"

"That's what we are trying to determine. They may be legitimate, or enough to be legitimate that it could be overlooked. We talked to Dallas, who wasn't happy."

"No, I didn't think that he would be. He has enough on his plate."

"Something is going on with him. I sense that he is searching for something, and not finding it. He needs to find another line of work."

"Why would you say that?" Buckley waited, knowing that Locklin would speak when she was able to.

"I don't know. It's just that he has a look that he's haunted by something or someone. Does he have a girlfriend?"

"Not that I know of." Buckley suddenly groaned. "You realize that we have to face Charles and Lois tomorrow? That we can't avoid them?"

"I know. I've been praying about that. You have taught me to remember what my Dad did. That was to pray without ceasing."

"And you've reminded me. It's easy to forget, to slip into the mode that the world lives in. I have tended to do that lately."

"Maybe that's why we're going through what we are. To remind us that we need to trust God more and part of that trust is praying."

"It is, love." Buckley grew pensive. "You are happy here in the apartment?"

"I am." She shifted to look up at him. "I like that my friends are here but that we have our separate spaces. We're not in one another's faces. Your friends are here. This family here? It's closer than a normal family can be. Part of it is because you are all orphans and so are some of us ladies. There are enough others around to bring balance to our lives." She frowned. "Are you?"

"I am. I just wondered." Buckley dropped a kiss on her forehead. "Barnabas has asked what we want to change in decor. Paint. Flooring. Appliances. Furniture."

"He would do that? Of course, he would. I'm content for now. Other than all those little appliances that I don't know the name for." She grinned as he shook a finger at her before he reached to kiss her.

Chapter 41

Standing behind the pulpit the next morning, Buckley sought for Locklin, finding her sitting with Burnie and Breck on either side of her, near the back of the church. Breck had approached him, asking where he wanted Locklin to sit.

Buckley had stared at him and then stuttered out that he hoped she would be near the front, frowning as Breck shook his head.

"Not yet, Buckley. Not until we find the ones responsible. We want her near the back. That way, we can get her out of here as quickly as possible. The fellows want this for you."

He had finally nodded, agreeing with their logic. "Have you talked to her?"

"Not yet. We'll come to find her when you're done with your prayer before the service. She needs to be there with you."

"She does. She has expressed that plan." Buckley looked past Breck. "Locklin, love? Breck will come and find you when it's time for the service."

Locklin had stared at him before she turned questioning eyes towards Breck. "Protecting me? Who's on duty this morning?"

Breck had grinned. "This morning, Burnie and myself. We will be sitting with you in church until this is over. And it will be at the back of the church."

"Of course, it will. I was going to suggest that. Buckley, the worship team leader is looking for you for prayer." Locklin simply reached for Buckley's hand, leaving Breck grinning at her.

There was the usual bustle and stir as the people settled themselves for the message. Buckley looked down at his notes, and then found Locklin's gaze once more. He frowned and then nodded. Lord, I'm going to be talking without notes this morning. You need to lead my words, given me what You want me to say.

Locklin stood beside him after the service, greeting his people. No, her people as well, she thought. How did this happen? She stiffened as she saw Charles and Lois approaching, stepping back just a bit so that she was slightly behind Buckley. He glanced down at her and then up as Charles spoke. He needed to be polite, he knew, but he also needed to protect his wife. He quickly moved them on, and then drew Locklin away, heading for his office and towards his friends who were waiting.

"Everything okay, Buckley?" Brennen stared past him, to find Lois watching them. "What's with Lois?"

"We are trying to get away from her, if you must know. Did Jaxcy talk to you?"

"She did. Come on, we can lock up for you. Out the back door, Buckley. I have the codes for the system. Head on out." Brennen and Brady walked through the building, locking things up and then standing outside as Brody approached them.

"Lois and Charles?"

"You've got it. We sent Buckley and Locklin on." Brennen was frustrated. "This isn't right. They shouldn't have to be running like this. Not from the church."

"No, they shouldn't." Brody pulled out his phone. "It's Emma. She just sent an email." He paled as he read it. "Did you know that Lois is Charles' second wife? That his first wife drowned?"

"No, I didn't. Wait!" Brady groaned. "And let me guess. Lois was on the scene when it happened."

"Emma implied that. She said she'd confirm that and let us know. We need to go talk to Buckley and Locklin."

"After lunch, Brody." Brady moved away. "I'm taking my lady out for lunch. We'll meet about three?"

"Sounds good."

Buckley stared down at the photo and then read the attached email before he looked up at Brody. "I know Emma. She's sure of this?"

"She is. She's sent it on to Dallas. This complicates things, Buckley. It also places you in a difficult position."

"It does. It means that the board has to confront the chairman and question him." Buckley rubbed at his forehead with his thumb and forefinger. "I don't see in here where she gives the name of Charles' first wife."

"She hasn't. She's working on confirming information on her, but she hinted that somehow it connected to Locklin."

"I wish this was over. She's had enough. And frankly, so have I." He sighed again. "I know, Brody, I know. You know what I mean. She's fretting and trying hard to hide it from me. I also worry about the church family, what could happen to them, if for some reason whoever it is decided to go after me when we're meeting."

"Don't resign, Buckley. You're where God has put you. Everyone is confident in that fact. We'll work through this."

"I know we will, but it's so hard. I feel like I am walking through this deep ravine with only the faintest of light reaching down, and that the path is strewn with so many rocks and stones and thistles."

"He knows, Buckley. You and Locklin are in our prayers." Brody's hand rested on his friend's shoulder as he did just that, prayed for his friend.

Buckley stood for a moment, his eyes on the picture, before he spoke.

"Who is she, Brody? Are we sure that she is dead?"

"What?" Brody spun from where he had taken a few steps away. "What are you saying, Brody?"

"What if she is still alive? Somewhere in the world? Look what happened to Jaxcy's parents. They were held for so many years overseas, both them and Jaxcy thinking the other was dead. What if she was removed, her death faked, and this Lois moved in? How long have they been married?"

"I don't know. I'll find that out." Brody was away to the computer that he favoured, booting it up, and beginning his search.

Buckley sighed. He needed to go speak with Locklin, but he knew that she was meeting with some of the ladies for prayer and Bible study. He would not disturb that, not unless it was an absolute emergency, and he didn't feel that it was. Not yet. It might come to that, but he wasn't ready to scare her. She needed the time with the ladies, for their support. They could relate to what she was going through, better than most.

His friends watched as he walked away before they exchanged glances, knowing it was at the point in the adventure that things could and would break loose. And they feared for their friend. They felt that he would face worse than they did, and from within the church he loved. And if that was the case, how would he continue as the minister that was just who they needed there?

Chapter 42

Looking around the kitchen doorway, a huge smile on her face, Locklin watched as Buckley entered, setting his shoes in the closet, and then pausing before he looked up. She frowned as she saw that his smile didn't reach his eyes.

"Buckley? Sweetheart?" She walked towards him and into his hug.

"Locklin, love. Have a good time with the ladies?"

"I did." She accepted his kiss before she hugged him, standing with her arms still around his neck. "You're troubled."

"I am. Brody received some information from Emma that we need to talk about."

"He did." She stepped back, her hand reaching to draw him to the kitchen. "Sit. I have your coffee and some Irish baking. Blair and Devaney were to Riverville yesterday and stopped in the Irish bakeshop. They brought back goodies for all of us."

"They did? It's the wife of one of Abe's lifelong friends who has it." He sat, a sigh rising from him. "Sit, Locklin, with your tea. We'll talk of other things, then spend time in prayer. We are going to need it."

Locklin finally reached for Buckley's hands, finding his chilled. "Buckley, how bad is it?" They had spent time in prayer, seeking protection and wisdom.

"It's bad, love. Lois is Charles' second wife, and we don't know that his first wife is even dead. Emma's looking into that."

Locklin nodded. "That's what we discovered. We were talking about it this morning. Fynn digs deep, and she will, given that she likes that kind of thing. I still want to see her building with all her creepy-crawlies."

"And you will. What did she find out?"

"That Lois is indeed Charles' second wife. She talked to some of the older people in the church, who could remember things. No, we weren't gossiping. They want this over for you. Some of them have never really trusted her."

"They haven't? That's interesting. Nothing has ever been said to me."

"And they won't. They have no proof. Without proof, it's just gossip. Anyway, Fynn is able to draw them out. Guenivere was with her. The consensus is that his first wife just disappeared. She is reported to have drowned in the lake, caught in the undertow, but no one found her body."

"It would be easy to have placed her on a freighter, the freighter work its way through the canal, and then down the St. Lawrence River and to the ocean. From there, they could go anywhere. It sounds so much like Jaxcy's parents."

"It does. Jaxcy was intending to speak with her parents. To see if they had heard of any female on a neighbouring island that might be her." She paused, to sip at her tea, her finger running along the edge of the cup when she replaced it on the saucer. "Where does that leave Charles?"

"In a lot of trouble, unless he is cleared. What else, Locklin? I know there is more."

Locklin sighed. "There is, sweetheart. Dallas was around just before you came in. He wanted to clarify some things from my past. The forces are planning on moving in shortly, to clear up the drug houses and dealers both here and at home. He warned me that we will need to be extra cautious."

"And we will be. I just want this over." Buckley sighed, running a hand through his hair. "I keep saying that. I know that's what the others said as well."

"And it will be, Buckley. It will be. It is God's timing, not ours. He has plans for this, that we don't know about."

"He does, love. He brought me you." He reached to kiss her, not wanting to let her go, suddenly afraid for her. He looked around as he heard a tap at the door. "Were we expecting anyone?"

"Not that I am aware of." Locklin moved to the door, standing to stare out of the peephole before she opened it. "Barnabas. Bruce. Come in."

"Locklin. You look beautiful." Bruce grinned at her, Barnabas' father a favourite among the ladies for the father figure that he had become.

"Thank you, Bruce. Please? We're in the kitchen, although we could move to the living room or office."

"The kitchen is fine. Buckley, son. How are you?" Bruce greeted Buckley before moving to find his own mug of coffee.

Barnabas hesitated, his eyes on Locklin. "Locklin?"

"Barnabas? I know this is more than just a casual call. Find your coffee and we'll talk."

Chapter 43

Bruce paused as he studied the younger couple, Buckley in deep conversation with Barnabas, Locklin with her eyes on him, a frown on her face. He shook his head at her and she nodded.

"Buckley? I think Bruce wants to talk to you." Locklin had no problem interrupting the men.

"Oh? Sorry, Bruce. I can get carried away."

"I know you can. It's okay, Locklin. I expect that from these young fellows." Bruce shoved a file folder across the table towards them. "Here. Read this. And then we talk."

"Bruce?" Buckley nodded when Bruce refused to answer. "Just tell me. Is it good news or bad?"

"We think it's good news. It's up to you two how you look at it."

Buckley opened the folder, Locklin leaning against his arm, to find photos of both of them. Buckley looked up, finding Bruce watching him intently.

"Go on, Buckley. Read through it."

Buckley exchanged a look with Locklin and then began to read through the paperwork, hearing some exclamations from Locklin. He turned back and read through it before he looked at his bride, finding a look of wonder on her face.

"Bruce? What is this?" Buckley didn't look at the older man.

"This paperwork? It is from the Foundation board. We want to set up a new ministry, dedicated to those who are seeking to heal from violence or crime, or domestic abuse. We have been praying over this for many weeks. We decided that we would each pray for a specific couple to head it. Every single one of us came to our meeting three days ago with a single name. Yours and Locklin."

"What?" Locklin stared at him, then at Barnabas, and finally at Buckley. "I don't understand."

"What Dad is saying, Locklin, is there was complete consensus that they want you two to prayerfully consider moving on to this. We go no further until you two have had time to pray about it and consider all aspects of it. If you say no, that God wants you to stay with the church, then we move on to pray for another couple. If you say yes, you will take on this new challenge, then we move forward with it, and with the church to find someone to fill the vacancy. We are in no rush. We are moving forward with the plans and paperwork, and setting it up with the legal team. But until you accept or decline, it remains as it is. In the planning stages."

Buckley had to swallow hard. "I'm not sure what to say. I didn't expect this."

"No, son. You wouldn't. You're too humble to expect something like this. We have seen the growth that has occurred particularly over the last months that you have worked with and counseled your friends. We have seen the change in you as you and Locklin go through this, a maturity that we don't often see in someone your age. Both of you are blessed by God with gifts that will be used by Him wherever you decide to serve. Buckley, if you need counsel, I have spoken with a couple of pastors who are willing to meet with you as an individual or as a couple. That choice is yours." Bruce watched the couple closely, seeing how close to tears Locklin was. "How be we pray and then we'll leave, letting you start the process of praying and discussing this."

Buckley stood in his office thirty minutes later, staring down at the closed folder. He could hear Locklin singing softly to herself as she cleaned up the kitchen for the night. They had not felt like eating, neither one of them. Buckley finally went looking for her, finding her curled up on the couch in the living room, staring at the fireplace that she had lit. He had laughed at her one day when she said she would use it whenever she wanted, that she found it relaxing.

"Locklin, love?" She leaned against him, welcoming his arms around her.

"I was not expecting this, sweetheart. Were you?"

"Not in my wildest dreams. You know, Dad and I had discussed something like this years ago, that someone needed to start this. I think that if he had not died, he would have. But Bruce is right. We have the experience of sorts that we need."

"We do. Unfortunately, we do." Her head on his shoulder, her finger rubbed at the black button of his flannel shirt. "They didn't give a time to let them know."

"No, they wouldn't. They are like that. They put forth something like this and then let God lead. It's how they are all. I think that's why they are so successful."

"I see." She looked up at him, watching his face closely. "What are your thoughts?"

"Right now? I'm stunned, I think. I certainly will pray about it. But unless we are agreed, we don't do anything. We have to agree on this."

"Thank you, sweetheart. I'm scared, I think, to move on. But I shouldn't be. I guess there has just been so much lately. In the last year, in fact."

"They know that, love. They know that and considered that when they discussed offering it to us." Buckley grew pensive, wishing his own father was there so that he could discuss it with him.

"Tomorrow's Sunday again. How do we face Charles and Lois?" Locklin finally spoke.

"The same we do every week. With a smile on our face and in God's strength. I don't know how people who have no faith get through times like this."

"I don't either. It's been hard, Buckley, so very hard. When I saw you that day, I ran towards you, praying that you would help me. If you hadn't, I don't know what would have happened to me."

"I am thankful that God sent me there. I just fear for what we might face. It's not over, but I sense that it will be soon. We need to pray for that hedge of protection, love."

"And I have been." Locklin grew quiet, finally dozing off, Buckley's head on hers.

Chapter 44

Locklin's steps slowed the next morning as she approached the church office. She could hear angry words and hesitated about approaching Buckley. She stepped to one side as Charles stalked past her, anger on his face. She frowned as she stared after him before she turned to find Buckley beside her.

"Buckley?"

He swept her into a hug. "I need you to stay close to me or one of the fellows today. Breck is bringing in some of our security guys. Charles seems to think that he is under suspicion. That's what that was all about. It's coming to a head, love."

"I know it is. He was angry and hurt." She looked back towards the door to the sanctuary. "What can he do to threaten your position?"

Buckley shrugged. "He can go to the board and then the congregation, try and make it seem that I am incompetent or evil or something. We won't worry about that now. Here, let's go meet the team for prayer. I really need it this morning."

Buckley paced through the gardens that afternoon, deep in thought. It had disturbed him that Charles had approached him like that. It was not him, he knew. What had happened that morning that set him off? He turned as he heard a throat clearing near him.

"Burnie?"

"Buckley, can we talk? I heard what happened this morning. I had come to find Locklin and overhead. I'm sorry. I didn't mean to." Burnie looked contrite and unsure of himself.

"It will soon go through the church. Charles threatened that." Buckley pointed to a bench and dropped down to it. "I can't stop it. I didn't ask for him to be investigated."

"No, his wife did, approaching Locklin the way she did and spreading around that she is Locklin's aunt." Burnie nodded at Buckley's look of surprise. "You didn't know that?"

"No, I hadn't heard that. And we know that's not true." Buckley sighed. "Now, where do we go? Charles will carry through with his threat. We can't stop him. If we did, it would look like we are trying to hide or cover up something."

"I know. You may need to leave the church that you love and that loves you. I pray that isn't the case. We have all grown under you so much, particularly with your messages on prayer."

"That was what God had laid on my heart. We need to be more like Christ when He prayed in the garden." Buckley grew silent. "I don't know what to do, Burnie. Locklin and I are praying through something right now. I feel as if I am on the edge of a cliff, ready to jump and it's too high for me to survive."

"That's an interesting way to phrase it. But it makes a good picture." Burnie looked around as he heard a sound. "Locklin, come on and join us. We're not talking about anything that you can't hear."

Locklin nodded, sitting beside Buckley, but the men could tell that she was upset.

"Love, what is it?"

"It's Lois. She showed up at our door. I didn't answer, but it was horrible what she was saying. She just kept banging on the door. I called security and they came and escorted her away." She looked at the two men. "She's accusing me of not being who I am. That I am an imposter and trying to corrupt you and the church." She blinked back her tears. "I'm not. She is."

"And we're proving it. I suspect that she knows, given what happened this morning." Buckley hesitated in what he needed to say. "It's going to get worse, love. We'll be in more danger, particularly you. You're the one that she seems to be going after. I don't understand why."

"This might explain it. Kataleen emailed me. I had just read it when Lois came to the door. Maybe if I hadn't I would have opened the door to her." She handed over her phone, the email ready to read.

Buckley read through it, drew in his breath, and then handed the phone to Burnie. Burnie read it and then read it again.

"We were right. His wife is still alive. How did Emma do that?"

"I don't know, but Abe is heading out to bring her home. Abe and his team. Where does that leave us now, Buckley? She'll be after us for sure. Her carefully crafted life is crumbling around her."

"It is. God will protect us, love. I don't know how or from what, but He will. Burnie, we need to get this to the others." Buckley reached for her phone. "I'll send it out as a group email and then we can meet. We are meeting, aren't we?"

"We are. The ladies are meeting with us as well." Burnie was on his feet, moving towards the building.

"Buckley? I'm so scared." Locklin crowded closer to him.

"You and me both, love. You and me both. This is getting out of hand." Buckley was on his feet, her hand in tight, rushing them back to the building. "We need to stay in here as much as we can. Barnabas will make sure that we have security with us if we need to be out."

"I sent the email on to Dallas. I wasn't sure if I should have."

"He needs to know. I would not be surprised if he knew already." Buckley paused outside the conference room door. "No matter what happens, Locklin, I love you more and more each day, more than I ever thought I could love someone. I don't want to see you hurt, but I am afraid."

"I love you too, sweetheart. We go forward, hand in hand, with God's protection. What He allows will happen."

Chapter 45

His heart in his mouth, Buckley ran from his car, heading for the building and racing up the stairs. He had been speaking with Locklin when he heard her scream and then silence. He hit the apartment door, flinging it open, not finding Locklin even though he searched. He stood, hand on his head, frantically looking.

The note of the back of the entry door caught his attention and he ran towards it, sliding to a halt and then pulling it loose. He opened it, his heart sinking as he realized that whoever was after them now had Locklin in their control. He would obey their directions but he had to let someone know. He snapped a quick picture of the photo, sending it on to Burnie, knowing that of all of them, he would be the one to receive the text the quickest.

Running for his car, Buckley sped away, not seeing Burnie waving frantically at him before Burnie ran for his car and followed him. Burnie frowned before he reached for the button on his steering wheel, calling Breck and telling him that he was following Buckley.

"Burnie, what are you talking about? Buckley's at the church."

"No, he's not. He was in their apartment. He sent me a copy of a note that was on their door. I'm following him." Burnie slowed as Buckley's vehicle slowed and then shot down a side road. "He's heading towards the old Wallace place."

"He is? That's one that Dallas has been looking at. Dear Lord, protect them." Breck was gone, hitting his own apartment door on the run, heading for the conference room. "Fellows, Locklin's missing. Buckley had a note on their door. Burnie's chasing him and will keep us up to where they are."

The fellows were on their feet, the ones who were there, rapidly following Breck as he ran for his truck, separating themselves into a few vehicles as possible.

"Baird's on duty?" Breck shot a glance at Bradon."

"He is. Pray that he's the one they call if paramedics are needed."

Breck slowed his truck and came to a stop behind Burnie. The men congregated around Burnie, questions flying at him.

"Whoa! Wait, guys!" Burnie's hands went up. "We need to move some of our vehicles. I don't think they can see us, but we can't take a chance."

"Have you called for Dallas?" Breck peered through the trees, towards the house. "Wait a moment! That's Charles and Lois' home."

"It is. Buckley has gone in. He was met by someone holding a rifle or something on him." Burnie was scared, he had to admit to himself. He had had to leave a voice mail for Dallas and then had opted to call Will, speaking with him. Will was on his way, he said, with patrol vehicles. He sternly ordered Burnie and whoever it was with him to stay put.

"Have you seen Charles or Lois?" Bradon stood beside Burnie, watching the house.

"I saw Lois. She appeared in the doorway after Buckley had gone in." Burnie turned, his phone in his hand. "I just got a text from Emma. Abe's home with Charles' first wife. She was correct in her supposition. The lady was kidnapped, taken to a freighter, and shipped overseas. Close to the island where Jaxcy's parents were. Emma can't find any evidence that the islands are connected. She did say the lady had been forced to be a cleaner in a drug lord's home."

"That's is what we thought." Breck looked around. "How long do we wait?"

"As long as it takes." Bradon turned and faced them. "We can't go in. We have to let the police go in. If we did, it would be seen as trespassing and they could shoot us. I'm sure that Will has all the help he needs."

Will approached the building fellows, shaking his head. Of course, they would all be there. It was what they did.

"Any sign of them?"

"Not since they took Buckley in." Burnie pointed to the front door. "They walked him in through the front door. Lois came out just after and was looking around. I have not seen any sign of Charles."

"No? Okay. I want you all to stay right here. We're moving in. The judge has signed off on warrants for us. So it will be all legal." Will was away, heading for Dallas and the waiting officers.

The fellows watched as the police moved in. Lois appeared briefly at the door before she tried to slam it back shut in their faces. The police moved in. The fellows prayed as they had not for a while, not knowing what condition that their friends would be in, or even if they would be alive.

Dallas and Will moved quickly through the two-story house, searching. Lois screamed at them that they had no right to be there, that they were intruding on her, until she was handcuffed and removed, a stern warning given her and the search warrants shown to her.

"Where are they, Will?" Dallas was puzzled. They had searched the house. "They have to be here."

Will looked around. "You know, this house was rumoured to have belonged to a bootlegger. It's that old. There were tunnels running to the lake and secret rooms, or so it's told. Let's start searching for that. Find out who would know."

Will was away, down to the basement, officers with him to spread out, searching. Dallas was frustrated. He hadn't been able to find anyone who could verify the rumours. At a shout from one of the officers, he ran for the stairs, almost falling down them in his haste to descend. He met Will running his way.

"Where?"

"In the root cellar." Will slid to a halt on the dirty concrete in the room. "Of course, it would be in the root cellar. Here, let's get that door open. Break it down if you have to."

A few solid kicks from many feet had the door splintered enough that it could be pulled away from the frame. The officers in protective gear went first, shouts rising in the air for the men they found to halt and raise their hands. Will and Dallas followed, their hearts dropping as they saw Buckley bound hand and foot on the floor, trying to move but unable to do. They followed his line of sight and then were across the room, dropping to their knees beside Locklin, cries for help sounding from them.

Chapter 46

Turning to call for paramedics, Will moved swiftly towards Buckley even as an officer's knife sliced through his bonds. Will restrained him from moving towards Locklin.

"I have help coming, Buckley. What happened?"

Buckley shook his head. "I don't know. She was like that when I found her. I didn't have a chance. They had me down and bound before I could get to her." He was almost sobbing as he watched Brady and his partner, Patrick, appear and then begin to work on Locklin. "They said they had given her something. An overdose."

Patrick spun at his words. "An overdose? With what?"

"I don't know." Buckley didn't feel the tears that were running down his face. "They didn't say, just said an overdose."

Patrick was on his feet, running for the rig, grabbing the kit that he needed, with the medication that he prayed would save Locklin's life.

"How long, Buckley?" Brady's sharp voice cut through the silence. "I don't know. I was here for fifteen or twenty minutes before they forced me down here. They said it was just before that. Please, Brady?"

"I know, Buckley. We're working on it." Brady and Patrick exchanged glances even as Brady spoke.

"We need to move, Brady." Patrick was reaching for Locklin, to help transfer her to a stretcher. "Will, we're off. An escort?"

Will pointed to two officers. "In front and back. Now move. Buckley, no, we'll get you there. Just let them move." Will's hand on Buckley's arm stopped him from moving forward. "Dallas, you've got this. I'm with Buckley."

Will's hand on his arm propelled Buckley up the stairs, through the house to the outside and then to Will's car. He was shoved roughly inside before Will was behind the wheel, lights flashing and sirens blaring as he raced after the ambulance. He could see the building fellows scattering and gave a grim smile as he saw them pulling in behind him. He lost them on the race to follow Locklin, but he knew that they would be there, for Buckley, just as he had been there for them.

Doc looked around as the charge nurse hurried his way.

"Doc, we have an overdose coming in. Brady and Patrick are on their way in. Brady asked that we tell you that it's Locklin."

"Locklin? There is no way that she would do this on purpose. She doesn't do drugs. Clear room 1." Doc was on the move, heading for the ambulance bay.

"Already done. Our people are ready, Doc. Brady also asked that you be told Will Peters was heading this way with Buckley."

Doc helped pull the doors to the rig open, even as Brady and Patrick reached for the stretcher.

"She's starting to code, Doc. I don't know if we got to her in time." Patrick was standing on the bars of the stretcher, his hands working to perform CPR even as the stretcher was rushed in a rapid manner to the room.

"Keep it up, Patrick. Sue, heart monitor. Brady, do we know what it was?"

"No, we don't. They told Buckley what they had done, but not with what." Brady's hands were busy, starting the IV line and then reaching for the defibrillator. "We need this. Patrick, here."

They watched as Locklin's body jerked with the electric shock sent through her. And it was repeated.

"We have rhythm, people." Doc's rapid orders were followed, the debris from needles and other equipment flying through the air.

An hour later, Doc finally stepped back. Locklin had been intubated and was still on the heart monitor. He watched closely, finally nodding.

"We did it, people. We did it. She's still alive and steady. Brady, Patrick, thank you. Now off with you two. I know it's after your shift."

"We would have stayed, no matter who it was. You know that, Doc."

Doc nodded and then turned, fatigue weighing him down. He had called in an extra physician to cover the busy Emergency Department even as he fought for

Locklin's life. She was stable, he knew, but for how long? She could regress, that he knew. But for now, he'd send her to the ICU, find Buckley and then go home and hug his Anna. He needed that. It had been a brutal day, too many accidents. Losing the young mother and her small son had been hard, harder even to talk with the young husband.

Breck was watching for Doc, seeing the fatigue in his steps as he approached. He walked towards him, trying to assess his mood.

"Doc?"

Doc looked up, a hand rising to tap Breck's shoulder. "Where is he?"

"We found an empty room and have him in there. He was looked over. Rope burns on his wrists. He was bound and couldn't get to Locklin."

"Was he? All right. Let's go find him."

Pausing just inside the doorway, Breck's hand resting this time on his shoulder, Doc watched as all the faces turned his way. He could see that Will was still there, in a chair beside Buckley. Buckley sat, not looking around, his form crumpled and grieving, Doc could tell. Brody moved from the seat beside him, to let Doc sit.

Doc waited for Buckley to look up, a prayer on his lips for his young friend.

"Buckley?" He drew in a breath as Buckley raised his head.

"She's gone, isn't she? They don't survive overdoses. Not after that long."

"She's alive, Buckley." Doc waited for Buckley to hear him and then he repeated his words. "She's alive, Buckley."

Buckley's eyes shot to Doc. "She is? She's still alive?" He could barely get the words out.

"She is, Buckley. She crashed on the way in from the ambulance, but with Patrick and Brady's help and the staff here, we were able to revive her. She's intubated right now and on a heart monitor. But she is alive."

Buckley's eyes slid closed. "I was afraid, Doc, afraid that I had lost my heart. Can I see her?"

"Give us a few moments to get her situated in her room. Then we'll come to get you." Doc stood, his eyes on Buckley before he spoke to everyone in the room. "Locklin is still with us. God worked His healing touch there. She is still not out of danger, but she is alive." Doc paused for a moment before he walked away, a heaviness to his steps. No, there was no guarantee that Locklin would even make it, despite what they had done.

Chapter 47

Buckley haunted the ICU for three days, not willing to leave to sleep, to shower, or to even eat. His friends made sure that he was taken care of but he just shook his head and walked away if they even suggested that he leave. Barnabas had been around on the third day, worried about Buckley, finding him standing in the middle of the waiting room, staring into space.

Barnabas touched his arm lightly and then grasped it to lead him to a seat.

"Sit, Buckley. You're going to fall over if you don't." Barnabas watched with compassion as Buckley sank down, dejection, worry, and sorrow in his bearing. "How is she?"

"They've been able to take the ventilator off. She's on room oxygen but she'll go back on it if she can't keep her oxygen levels up. Why, Barnabas? Do we even know why?"

"I'm not sure that all the pieces are together yet. I haven't talked to Dallas today. He said that he was around last night."

"He was. He didn't say much." Buckley sat back, scrubbing his hands down his face. "Where do I stand with the church?"

"What do you mean?"

"What I said. Where do I stand? I'm sure the board will want me out with Locklin overdosing even though it was done to her."

"No, that's not what they've said. Charles resigned from the board and left the church. Edward Styles took over. They are meeting nightly to pray for you two. He wanted me to tell you to take the time that you needed. This was not your fault or doing."

"He said that? I still don't know if I can go back and preach again." Buckley sighed. "Maybe this is God's way of telling me to move on."

"It might be but don't make any decisions without prayer, talking to us, and talking to Locklin. I have every confidence that she will heal. We're praying for a touch of the Master's garment for her."

"Thank you." He looked up to see Dallas standing in front of him. "Dallas? You're back. That can't be good."

"Actually, Buckley, it is. I just wanted to update you. Locklin?"

"She's improving, they tell me. I don't see it." Buckley rubbed at his sore, red eyes. He had wept too much, he thought, ready to weep some more. "You're here." He repeated himself without meaning to.

Dallas nodded. "I am, Buckley. I have a photo to show you." He opened the portfolio that he had set on the chair beside him. "Take a look at this photo."

Buckley finally reached for it, blinking rapidly. He frowned. "That's Locklin's father, isn't it?"

———

"It is. We have received word and have confirmed it that it was not her father who was shot and killed at the courthouse. The police are working on identifying that man. He was close enough in looks and had her father's identification on him." Dallas tapped the photo. "This is her father. We have traced him to a property in Quebec. The authorities are moving in on it as we speak."

"He's alive?" Buckley was stunned. "He's been alive all this time."

"Yes. We'll have to get his statement and that will take time. Once we can get him cleared and back here, I'll talk to Locklin."

Buckley slumped back against the wall. "So, what has been the point of all this?"

"Locklin? We suspect that she was being used against her father. If he shut up and didn't say anything, then she would be safe. But the rumblings that we have heard from someone undercover is that he is starting to rebel and make noise, threatening to run. He's been put under harder lockdown from what we can determine."

"What about Lois? Where does she fit in?" Barnabas watched Buckley closely, seeing how near to collapse that he was.

"She's related to the drug lord in South America. She has refused to talk but others who worked for her have. They are getting ready to arrest him in that country. That should happen today."

"Charles?"

"He was innocent or so he claims. We're still talking with him. We have him under house arrest at the moment. His first wife has returned but wants nothing to do with him. The Foundation lawyers are working with her."

"That's good. Find her someone to talk with." Buckley was on his feet, moving towards the ICU units, without saying another word.

"He's shutting down, Barnabas." Dallas watched him walk away.

"He is. But there is nothing that we can do. Not until he collapses. He'll hold himself up as long as he can."

"Locklin?"

"She's recovering. He won't say much. He's losing his hope, Dallas."

"I see that. I need to run. Keep me updated. I'll be back around as soon as I have more word on her father."

Buckley stood beside Locklin, his hand on her cheek, his heart still even though he knew he should pray. He just didn't have the words he needed. But God knew, Buckley thought. This is when the Holy Spirit prays for us.

Chapter 48

A week later, Locklin curled up once more on their couch, glad to be home, but still struggling to recover. She had been given a list of symptoms to watch for. She had read it over and then tossed it on the kitchen counter. Refusing to acknowledge it, Locklin had simply shut her mind to the possibilities. God was healing her, she thought. That is all that mattered.

Fynn watched her carefully from where she sat near her.

"Locklin?"

"Fynn?"

Fynn grinned at her. "We need to plan a date when you can come play with my creepy crawlies."

"We do. I just wish that this had never happened." Locklin didn't look up as Buckley sat beside her. "It's taken too much from me, too much from Buckley."

"It takes from all of us, but you two in particular, it has taken a lot." Fynn was not sure how to continue. "God kept you alive, Locklin. I don't know why. But He loves you both. Let me pray with you and then I'm leaving. You two need to talk."

Buckley rose to follow her to the door, locking it behind her, a hand resting against it, in what seemed to have become a favourite position of his. He looked over his shoulder. He had asked that he be the one to tell Locklin that her father was still alive, had been returned to this area, but was still being debriefed, as they put it.

"Buckley?" Locklin studied him as he sat beside her, sweeping her into a hug and then just holding her.

"Locklin? Are you sure that you should be up?"

"For now. What is going on?"

"Locklin, Dallas approached me a week ago. He handed me a photo." Buckley reached for the envelope he had set down on the end table. "This is it. Before you look at it, we need to pray."

Locklin finally reached for it, puzzlement on her face. Pulling open the envelope, she then extracted the photo. A hand went to her mouth as she blinked rapidly. "It's Dad. Oh! It's Dad." Then she frowned. "But, Buckley, the date. It has to be wrong."

"No, love, it's not. The man who was killed testifying in Toronto? They have finally determined that it was not your father. I don't know all the details and I am not sure that we will as it was an undercover officer who contacted the force there. Your father was held in Quebec."

"He's been alive all this time? So close and yet so far. How is he? Where is he?" Locklin's words tumbled over each other.

"He's as well as can be expected. He's receiving treatment. And he is in the area. They're still talking with him. The police do not want you two together for a few more days. Not until they can make all their arrests."

"He's here? Oh, Buckley! Dad is alive and here? Now, I can heal! But I want to see him!"

Buckley hugged her tighter. "You will, love. You will. Barnabas has the Foundation lawyers and some others working with him."

Locklin snuggled down against her husband, wiping at her face. "I am suddenly so tired. That's not right."

Buckley gave a soft laugh. "Yeah, it is. You're recovering from dying. You did die, you know."

"I know. Brady talked to me about it. He was so scared, he said. He didn't want to have to face you if I didn't make it back."

"I would not have blamed him. I blame the ones who did this to you."

"What happened with Charles and Lois?"

"Charles has been removed from here. They moved him somewhere to protect him until he can testify. Lois? Let's just say that God has avenged so many people. Somehow she managed to get some drugs and overdosed. They didn't find her in time."

"That's so sad. What about his first wife?"

"She's given her statement and then moved on. She divorced Charles. She has a lot of healing to do. And no, neither lady was related to you. Lois apparently made that up, to try and get close to you. She's been playing everyone for years."

———

"That's sad. What drives people to that?"

"Greed. Money. Lust." Buckley's voice had softened as he felt Locklin's body relaxing. He was content, for the moment, to sit and hold her, and spend time in prayer. He eventually reached for her Bible, opening it to read the passages that he loved on prayer.

Chapter 49

Three weeks later, feeling mostly recovered, Locklin moved restlessly around the rose garden. Something was up, she could tell, something that no one seemed to want to share with her. She shrugged, not willing to push it. Life was too precious, she decided. She jumped as arms surrounded her and she felt the familiar beard brush her face as a kiss landed on her cheek.

"Buckley, that had better be you."

Buckley's deep laugh caused her to smile. "It is, love. It is. I was looking for you."

"You were? Well, you found me. What did you want?"

"I want you to turn around but keep your eyes closed." She could hear the joy and laughter still in his voice.

"Really? My eyes closed? And why?" She was laughing as she questioned him.

He laughed with her. "Just humour me? Please? Okay, I have your hand. Your eyes are closed. Trust me, love. I won't let anything harm you. Okay. We're stopping right here. Now, when I ask you to, I want you to open your eyes. Yes, love, I need you to drop my hand."

Buckley watched her closely before his quiet voice whispered in her ear. "You can open your eyes."

Locklin blinked as she did so, the few moments that she had her eyes closed causing the light to be too bright. She looked around, her gaze coming back to the man who stood five feet in front of her, a bouquet of yellow roses in his hand. Locklin's hands covered her mouth, even as she blinked rapidly to clear the tears.

"Dad! Dad! It's you? It's really you? Oh, Daddy, how I missed you." Locklin was across the few feet, her arms around her father's neck even as his arms surrounded her, the roses dropping to the ground. She sobbed even as her father wept.

Buckley blinked back his own tears. It had been God who had spared them, he thought, and brought them back together. Logan had a lot of healing to do, that he had admitted, but to be near his daughter? That was all he had asked. Buckley had met with him and Dallas the day before, making the arrangements for him to move into one of the spare apartments in the building, just until he was healed enough to know where he wanted to live. He nodded at Barnabas who had walked with the two men to find Locklin. Barnabas gave a small wave, heading off to find the building family.

Locklin finally stepped back, leaning against Buckley, taking the roses that her father handed her. He had always given his wife yellow roses and for him, there was no other colour to give his beloved daughter. They spoke for a while before the three of them moved towards the building, finding all the fellows and the ladies waiting for them. Barnabas had arranged for that.

Locklin wandered the lobby, her arm linked with her father, introducing him, telling him bits and pieces of the fellows and ladies. She prayed that he would not be overwhelmed, but was so glad to have him nearby. Doc had approached her, letting her know that he would be checking in on her father, just to be sure that he was okay. Doc had hugged her and then walked away, wiping at his eyes, complaining that he had dust or something in them. No one believed him, knowing the soft heart that Doc had.

Late that night, Locklin found Buckley on the balcony, just watching the stars. She cuddled close, her emotions still raw.

"Thank you, Buckley. I think you prayed Dad home."

"We all did, love. We all did. Burnie admitted to me today that he never felt it was your father. I think he was putting out feelers all along."

"Bless Burnie. He needs to find a lady."

"It will take a special lady for him. You have to be careful around him. You just might end up in a book."

"Is that right? I feel like we have lived a mystery story or a police drama or something. But God was there, just as you said."

"He was, love." Buckley stooped to kiss her. "Have I told you today how much I love you?"

———

"You have, and I never tire of hearing that. I love you, too. I just never expected to be a minister's wife."

A month later, Locklin was on the hunt for Buckley. She had searched for him at the church, and then through the building, finally tracking him down in the rose garden. He reached out a hand to draw her to the bench with him.

"Missed me?" He laughed as she swatted at him.

"Always. I just needed to ask you something but I can't remember what." Locklin snuggled down against him. She never grew tired of being held, finding his love just what she needed to help her heal, that and his prayers.

"It can't be important if you don't remember."

They sat, watching the sun set, throwing out the rose and purple streamers over the lake. They had made a decision about what they wanted to do but were still praying it through.

"I guess that we need to talk to Barnabas and Bruce." Locklin finally broke the silence.

"I guess that we do. You're sure?"

"I am. God led us through things to give us the knowledge to help others. He had brought others into contact with us who will help." Locklin looked up at him. "I'm scared, Buckley."

"Me, too. This is jumping off into the unknown, isn't it? But God will guide us. I will miss the church and it's people."

"So will I. Even though I'm not a minister's wife." Locklin laughed at the face he made. "I'm not."

"Yes, you were. And you are so suited to this new venture." He stood, a hand reaching for hers, helping her to stand, then bowing his head to pray for them.

Barnabas looked at them as he opened his door.

"Come in. I wasn't expecting you. Mom and Dad are here. They'll be glad to see you. Mom was asking about you, Locklin. And you're in time for a meal."

Laughter and conversation helped to ease the nervousness that Locklin was feeling. She looked up at Buckley as she helped to clear away the meal, finding him watching her and then nodding.

Bruce had been watching the young couple closely and then nodded himself. They have reached a decision. I guess, then, Lord, we'll be putting our plans for the new ministry on hold.

"Dad, how be we head for the living room with our coffee for the men and tea for the ladies? Mom, you had that tray of sweets?"

"I do. Now, find those little glass plates that were your grandmother's. We need them. I feel like we're going to be celebrating. She always used them for that."

Barnabas merely grinned, digging out the plates that his mother wanted. He watched as the ladies were seated and served and then sat himself, his eyes on Buckley and Locklin.

"Dad? Will you lead us in a time of prayer? I think we need it."

"I agree, son. Now, any special requests?" Bruce's eyes twinkled as he asked that.

"Not really, Bruce." Locklin reached for Buckley's hand. "But I do appreciate your prayers."

Thirty minutes later, their heads raised and conversation and laughter flowed among the five before Bruce took a chance and broke into the conversation.

"I think you have something to tell us, Buckley. I don't think you ended up here for just a visit."

Buckley shook his head, his hand reaching for Locklin's.

"We do. Just bear with me for a moment. Locklin, when I saw you running towards me that day, I could do nothing else but step in. I didn't realize what an adventure we would end up on. I certainly never expected to find the love of my love that way. God was good. He protected you from Hall and brought him to justice. He also protected you and myself over the weeks that we struggled to make sense of everything.

"With you not having your memories when we married, I always felt that you were short changed. But you never let it or seldom let it come between us. I love the lady that you are becoming. You are my Proverbs 31 lady. Mom and Dad would have loved you.

"To find out that your father was alive and to have reunited you two? That is an answer to a prayer I don't think we asked. God moved there. Your father has healing to do, as do you. But we're working on that." He stopped for a moment, overcome with his emotions.

Bruce nodded. "You two are a testimony to your faith. Buckley, I hear that your messages are reaching and changing people. But what is it that you wanted to say?"

Buckley looked down at Locklin and swallowed hard. They were confident in their decision but now that the time had come to give it, he wasn't so confident.

"A while ago, you approached us, asking us to consider a new ministry that the Foundation was planning. You asked us to take the time to pray it over and when we had made a decision to come and find you. We have made that decision." Buckley raised his eyes, searching the faces of the three in front of him. "We have tendered our resignation to the church board. We are accepting the new ministry that the Foundation offered us. Going through what we did? We both feel that God led us through that, to give us some understanding of what is needed. I can no longer just serve in a church. And Locklin keeps reminding me that she is not a minister's wife."

Bruce nodded. "No, she's not but she is fitted for her new role. Thank you, Buckley, Locklin, for accepting this. It's a position that will grow and grow, we suspect. We will need to meet but first, let's spend some time in prayer."

Locklin walked back through their apartment late that night, not really heading anywhere in particular, and ran into Buckley as he stood watching her.

"You're sure, Buckley?"

"I am. And you?"

"I am. I mean, I'm scared, nervous, excited, not sure about what emotion to have."

"Bruce was right. You are suited to this new duty. And I feel the same as you. Let's spend some time in prayer. Tomorrow is Sunday, and Edward said that he would read our resignation after the service. This will be hard."

"It will be, but God is leading us on to different ministries. I have a vision when Bruce was praying for us. That this ministry started here and then kept expanding, town by town."

"God will lead in that, love." He bent and kissed her, wrapping her tight in his arms.

Thank you for choosing the story of Buckley and his love, Locklin. They had an adventure that I had not planned on. Once more, they just took over the story and kept on going. It was not planned that Locklin have amnesia. They threw that in to move the story along. I love it when characters just take over. Mine always do. We call them unruly characters, who did not share the story and just take over the steering wheel.

Prayer? How do we pray? When do we pray? Only when we need something? Only when something prompts us to? When we think of someone that we promised to pray for?"

We are exhorted in Scripture to pray without ceasing. For me, that means a day-long conversation with God. He wants to hear from us, hear our joys and sorrows. He knows them already but we need to vocalize them to Him. I often turn to the passage in John, where Christ prayed in the garden. Just to think that He prayed for each one of us all those years ago. That is something to meditate on.

Drugs are becoming more and more dangerous. It has become common for emergency personnel to carry the antidote, but even then, it is sometimes too late. My heart goes out to those who have lost loved ones to drugs and to overdoses.

And of course, Abe and his men and their ladies had to return. I am always happy to see them, even though they drop in unexpectedly. Their stories are in the *His Guardians* series. And the Irish bakery? That is Dave and Rylee, whose story is *A Touch of His Garment*.

Buckley is well loved by his friends. He needed a special lady to love. And Locklin needed that special fellow. I think that they found one another. Love at first sight? Sure, I believe in that. But this is a book, which gives me the opportunity to have that happen. Nothing was planned, really, for them. For Buckley to move from the church that he loved to a new ministry, something totally new and untried? Not in the planning, but it added to the story, giving another dimension to his character.

God bless each one of you.

Ronna